Dark Heart of Ilmoure

Cara N. Delaney

I

The bus was decidedly less comfortable than the train had been, though it at least wasn't crowded. Barely half a dozen passengers, none of whom had said a word to her as she'd walked past to take a seat in the back. Plenty of surreptitious stares, though. Like they were offended by her very presence. She'd even had to ask around to find the right bus in the first place – it had no sign, nor indeed a single clue, advertising its destination. To Iris, it very much felt like Ilmoure had simply fallen off the map since the last time she'd seen it.

It shouldn't have been surprising, she reasoned as she tried to focus on the open book in her lap again. Since the mine had closed, the town's reliance on tourism had been decidedly at odds with its unwillingness to accommodate even the smallest of necessary changes. Where the other towns along the coastal road had grown and adapted, Ilmoure had stayed the way it had always been. Most people had insisted that this merely created a rustic charm. The years in Durham had shown Iris very plainly that it was simply good, old-fashioned stubbornness. Now the town was paying the price for it.

Looking out the grimy window every now and again, she watched the scenery slowly change. Today, the ocean was as flat and lifeless as she'd felt the day she'd received the letter. Addressed to *Ms. Iris Grey*, as formal as could be. Unlike the previous two invitations to visit home, which she had read and proceeded to ignore. This one, she couldn't simply put away until she forgot about it. As much as she loathed returning to the place she'd left in a storm so long ago, she wanted to be there for Laura.

Just for a few days, she'd promised herself. Then she would be free once more. The more time had passed, the more certain she was that leaving had, in fact, saved her from a life of misery. Even if it had caused some wounds in the process – both for herself and others. Perhaps she worked long hours now, and perhaps she had traded the townhouse for two rooms and access to a bathroom down the hall – but they were hers, and her mother could just cry about what she liked to do in there.

Which lately hadn't been all that much, but Katherine didn't know that, and Iris felt a dark amusement at the idea of letting her wonder and fret and get mad about it. She sighed and tried to squash it. She'd have to meet them, after all, and a funeral was not the time or the place for a scene.

The bus turned with a jolt, veering away from the coast. The road through the hills was narrow, much less well maintained, and made the rest of the journey a rather uncomfortable affair. With no small amount of relief, Iris watched as they passed the town sign.

Welcome to Ilmoure – City of Gold

The washed-out yellow letters were as faint a memory of that as the town itself. The mine had run dry so long ago, nowadays the only gold you could find was around the necks of the town's self-proclaimed ladies whose husbands hadn't lost their entire fortunes just yet.

Near the town hall, the rickety old bus finally stopped.

"End of the line."

Like Iris hadn't known that. She slid out of the bench, took her travel bag from underneath her seat and made her way to the front of the bus.

"Is this where I board for the return trip?"

"It is. Every Friday, eight o'clock sharp. That is morning, not night."

Iris frowned. "The brochure said Tuesday and Friday."

"Every Friday," the driver repeated. "I don't make the schedule."

"Then who does?"

"Company back in Durham. Are you getting off or what?"

Iris swallowed a reply and nodded. The handle of her bag cut into her palm as she descended the creaky steps, until she convinced herself to relax her fingers when she stood on solid ground again. No use. Even if she contacted the company, chances were she would get nowhere. If anyone even answered.

She'd be stuck here for another week.

She tried to compose herself before she turned to look around. Not much had changed. Perhaps the pavement looked a little darker. Maybe the market square was a little too empty for the time of day. Maybe the windows looked a little more dull. A few of them were nailed over. But the townhall remained as grand as it had always been. The general store still had the same pink begonias in front of its display window. And the hotel across the square still displayed the hammer, shovel and mine cart that had once symbolised the town's pride and joy.

It also had a large, slightly faded sign next to the double doors announcing that it would close down eight months ago.

Iris stared at it, wondering which deity she had unwittingly offended, and how she could make amends and receive a little miracle in return. One of the things that had swayed her to go and not just throw the letter away had been the prospect of limiting contact to a few hours at a time, and otherwise being unbothered in her own hotel room. Perhaps she should have sent a telegram ahead, just to make sure. But who would expect one of the oldest businesses in town to simply close up shop like that?

With a deep sigh, she turned away from the hotel. Perhaps she could stop by Mrs. Hamish's boarding house later. Someone in this town still had to rent out rooms, right? For now, though, she'd have to make do. Her mother was expecting her.

II

A s she made her way through the streets, Iris couldn't help but notice all the empty windows. Not only shops. Houses, too, with the shutters closed and little piles of dust and debris collecting on the front steps. The snide, petty part of herself couldn't help but smile grimly at the sight. For all the scoldings she'd endured for wanting to move away, it seemed like she was far from the only one to leave and never return.

When she turned onto Folsom Street though, the stark difference surprised her. Even though there were dirty windows and facades dulled by time here, too, other houses looked freshly renovated. So did her childhood home. Better than when she had left it, she mused as she approached. The door and windows had received a fresh coat of paint. The iron lattice supporting the roses that were creeping up the wall was shiny and new. When Iris climbed the stairs, she found the door knocker to be welded to its plate. After a moment of confusion, she found the new doorbell set into the stone of the wall.

The splendour was almost startling after the dreary rest of the town. Like this one slice of it had somehow escaped the touch of decay, and grown fat and happy as if nothing had ever changed.

Unlike the resonating *clang* of the brass knocker, the bell's sound was barely audible from outside. Uneasy, Iris waited. Had anybody heard? Were they even home? Had they decided they didn't want to see her after all?

Iris tried hard not to reason that this must be it, and that she was free to leave. Maybe they had decided that whatever had moved them to invite her wasn't that important. Maybe they'd changed their minds, and now they-

When the door clicked and swung open on silent hinges, Iris nearly tripped backwards down the stairs. Dressed in stark black and white, a young woman she'd never seen before studied her.

"Yes?"

Iris steadied herself, one hand on the iron handrail. "Good day. I'm here for the funeral."

The woman stayed where she was, still as a statue until she spoke. "The funeral for Mr. Matthew is tomorrow."

"I am aware." The next words were barbs in her throat. "I'm family. Iris Grey. My mother is expecting me."

The way the woman studied her, she might as well have been a stranger from a most faraway land. Eventually, she nodded and stepped aside.

"Please come in. I will inform Mrs. Grey of your arrival."

She closed the door behind Iris and walked away, leaving her stranded in the hall. Iris smiled thinly. She should have known better than to expect hospitality.

As tempting as it was to go and take a seat in the salon, or even see if anyone was in the family room upstairs, Iris remained where she was. If she was stuck here for the coming week, it'd be best to make a good impression, to balance out the awful one she'd left the last time she'd been here.

The maid's heels signalled her return down the wooden stairs a few minutes later.

"Mrs. Grey and Mrs. Alden are expecting you."

Iris' heart beat in an erratic stutter before she managed to compose herself again. So Laura was here, too. Frankly, she should have expected that, and yet she was wholly unprepared for it.

A tangled mess of anxiety and stubborn pride settled in the pit of her stomach as Iris followed the maid upstairs. For all that she'd tried to stay in contact, she'd only ever received three letters back since she'd left, all from her mother. Including the invitation – summons, really – to attend the funeral of a nephew she'd last seen when he'd still been babbling in his crib. Did Laura even want to see her?

The family room hadn't changed much since she'd left. In fact, Iris couldn't tell if anything at all had been altered. Not even the furniture had been moved. The only things that had been rearranged were the family pictures. There was now a gap between the ones where they had been children, smiling into the camera without a care, and the ones that were framing their parents, an older Laura, and a wedding picture of her sister and Daniel Alden. The darkened patches of wallpaper were the only hint that there once had been more.

"Iris. How nice to see you."

Katherine Grey rose from where she'd sat in her armchair to greet her wayward daughter. The way she walked with measured steps, smiled and gestured at the sofa... Her whole demeanour was perfectly polite and pleasant. It hit Iris like a gut punch. She'd been prepared for a lot, from overly saccharine smiles to stern parental disapproval, even a repeat of their last rather noisy confrontation, but this perfect mask was worse.

Putting a smile on her own face was suddenly an almost insurmountable task.

"Hello, mother." With a lump in her throat, Iris looked between her and her sister, who had not risen from the couch. "Laura. It's..."

Good to be back. She swallowed the words before they could do more damage. It wasn't, for anyone here. So Iris went with the one thing she had to say before she'd be leaving solid ground with this conversation.

"I'm so sorry about Matthew."

Laura nodded stiffly. "Thank you."

And that was all. Iris waited, just a moment, if there would be more. Any sort of welcome. Laura stayed silent. It did give Iris time to notice something else. The reason why Laura wasn't on her feet.

She'd be burying her first child while carrying the second. Distant as they were, Iris' heart grew heavy at the idea. No mother deserved this.

"Please, sit down." Her mother glanced briefly at something behind Iris. "We will be having refreshments."

It felt much more like an order than it should, so Iris complied. The armchair was as uncomfortable as it had always been. It went well with the overall atmosphere. Iris bit the inside of her lip and decided not to mention that; they would hardly find it as funny as she did. Especially now.

The old clock in the corner accentuated the seconds until her mother spoke again.

"Did you have a pleasant trip?"

"It was fine." Iris folded her hands in her lap. "It's unfortunate they cancelled the Tuesday bus though."

"Did they." Katherine didn't sound surprised. "I'll be having your room prepared for the whole week, then."

Iris took a steadying breath. "Thank you, but that won't be necessary. I'll be getting a room."

This got the first emotion out of her mother – albeit not the one Iris had expected.

"Rent a room where?" Her smile was benign, but to Iris, it felt like derision. "The hotel has been closed for a while, last I heard. Poor Arthur, he was so proud of taking over the family business."

Iris' own smile was brittle. "Is Mrs. Hamish still renting out rooms?"

Her mother moved her hand in a dainty little wave. "The boarding house closed down just a year after you left." She inclined her head. "Really, it would be easier for you to stay with us."

The knot of anxiety twisted in Iris' stomach. "Are you sure? I wouldn't want to disrupt your day."

"We've been expecting you. Olivia will be taking your luggage upstairs."

And with that, the matter seemed to be taken care of, as far as her mother was concerned. Iris bit her tongue and decided not to argue. If the boarding house was closed, that left some of the sketchier private rentals near the pier, and if they hadn't substantially changed, they'd charge her a fortune for sleeping in a glorified crawlspace. She wasn't quite sure which would be worse, but staying in the family home would definitely be the cheaper way to suffer.

"I appreciate it."

Katherine simply nodded. The following silence was deafening. Seconds stretched like gum under a shoe. A saving grace was the maid bringing a tray of coffee. The minute she took to serve it allowed Iris something other to focus on than her crumbling expectations. Had so much changed after all? Had she missed something in the letters? A wish of reconciliation, now that the younger daughter was all but lost to the family?

Iris tried to find Laura's gaze. Her sister seemed perfectly content to ignore her presence, now that she had accepted Iris' condolences. Her mother was equally quiet until she dismissed the maid. Cup of coffee primly balanced on her knee, Katherine Grey was the picture of a hostess.

"So, Iris. I take it you are doing well for yourself?"

Her tone was pleasant, light, and nothing like she'd spoken to Iris in the last years before she'd left. Once again it threw Iris off balance, and she wasn't even sure why. It had been so long, she was almost over her own resentment. Was it so strange that her family had decided to let bygones be bygones, too?

"I am," Iris replied, just a tad too late. "Thank you."

Katherine nodded lightly. "Naturally. Are you still, what was it? Serving coffee?"

Iris shook her head. It made her a little dizzy. "No. I work at a book store now. The money is better, and it leaves me more time to write."

"Ah." So much that Katherine put into a single syllable, and none of it matched the joviality of her expression. "I see. You're still pursuing this... goal of yours, then?"

"I have been published." Iris took a sip of coffee. So weak that it was almost disgusting. "I could send you the magazines if you'd like."

"Oh, no need, dear. I'm sure I can find them in the library some time."

Head light and hand's suddenly clumsy, Iris managed a shaky smile. "Of course."

Why had she ever expected anything else.

The next excruciating hour was spent on the things she should have stuck to from the start. Superficial questions, idle gossip, and awkward silences. A question about the nature of Matthew's illness that was brushed off in a single, curt answer. Laura did not contribute another word to the conversation, leaving it up to Iris to attempt to fill the void.

When finally her mother put her cup back on the tray and called for the maid again, Iris would have jumped for joy, if she hadn't been feeling so utterly exhausted. Now, she had to make an effort not to slump, and to raise her feet when she followed the maid through the house. Up another set of stairs and to what had once been her childhood bedroom. When the maid named Olivia opened the door and ushered her inside, Iris was all but forced to take in the difference in the few moments it took her to cross the threshold. She hadn't taken much to Durham when she'd moved. She'd never expected to see any of it again, either. And yet, seeing a perfectly tasteful and completely featureless guest room where she was used to seeing overflowing bookshelves, an unmade bed and a messy desk was so jarring that it felt like she'd stepped into another world.

The maid put Iris bag down next to the bed and folded her hands in front of her.

"Dinner will be served at seven. I shall be fetching you when it is time."

Iris nodded a little belatedly, which seemed to be enough. The maid left with brisk steps, and the way the door clicked when it closed almost made Iris jump out of her skin. She pressed a hand to her stomach. It was fine. She was overreacting. It would be just fine.

If she told herself that enough times, she might just believe it.

III

I t took her barely a few minutes to unpack her bag. Afterwards, Iris spent an embarrassing amount of time pacing, looking out the window, and pacing some more. There was nothing left in the room to occupy her time. Asking what they had done with her things when they had changed the room – she was definitely not bold enough for that. In the end, Iris felt too wound up to stay inside the confines of the room. With a note on the vanity explaining that she'd be back before seven, she hurried downstairs and fled the house. Perhaps she should have found somebody to inform them, but that bore the risk of said someone wanting to accompany her. And right now, she needed the space.

And to think it had only been an hour. Iris wasn't sure if that should make her laugh or cry.

Outside, Iris hesitated ever so briefly before she turned her steps to the right and back towards the square. Passing by the still very stubbornly closed hotel, Iris took one of the many small streets down to the old pier.

In her memory, it was a lively, joyful place. Now, the storefronts she passed had dulled to vapid shadows of their original colours, half the windows nailed shut. The handful of people she passed spared her no greeting –

though Iris received some baleful looks. She hurried past them, trying to shake the feeling of eyes on her back.

Near the dry fountain, two stalls sat side by side, an elderly pair waiting for the inevitable. One of them still had scraps of signage left. If she wasn't mistaken, her father had bought her cotton candy from it every summer, until the year she had turned thirteen.

With a memory of pink sugar on her tongue, Iris turned away from the husks and continued on her path.

After the years in Durham, with its crowded shopping streets, loud nightlife, and the electric lamps that pushed back the shadows and extended days into nights, Ilmoure should have been... idyllic. Or so her friends had told her. How *nice* a vacation this would be. How *quaint* the place was. Iris had smiled and nodded and ordered a new round of drinks. She'd kept all the things Ilmoure wasn't to herself. No point in inviting questions she had no desire to answer.

A narrow alley led her away from what had once been a promenade. Here, people still lived their lives. Little stores were still open for local business. Cobblers, seamstresses, a barbershop. The post office, where she sent a telegram to her employer, hoping for understanding while offering to make up for the inconvenience with unpaid overtime. A short walk from there was the school where Iris had spent some miserable years yearning for the day she would be old enough to leave for university. Three houses down from that, the local library. Beyond, the intersection that led to the edge of town. Iris checked her pocket watch; she had plenty of time before she had to be back for dinner.

By all accounts, the woods and cliffs were lovely. Years ago, they had drawn tourists and locals alike for walks, picnics, sometimes family games in a clearing or by the side of the path leading up to the cliffs. Now, it was as quiet out here as it had been in the town itself. That suited Iris just fine. She took deep breaths of the fresh air, only now noticing how heavy she'd felt since she'd gotten off that bus.

At a split in the path, she slowed, unsure where to turn. Right, to the cliffs with the little benches and the view of Ilmoure and the ocean. They'd come up here so much, bringing a picnic basket and hoops to throw, and a firm leather ball to toss around. Laura had always been so bored with that, but she'd kept a smile on and played, for her little sister.

Abruptly, Iris turned to the left and onto the path leading into the woods.

It was cool underneath the trees, the sun filtering through the leaves not strong enough to warm the air just yet. The crisp air did wonders for her regardless, refreshing her and calming her at the same time. A smile crept on her face as she realised that she'd almost forgotten what that felt like. Even the most expansive and well-maintained parks in Durham couldn't compete with this.

The paths around Ilmoure were lined with little plaques displaying the names of wealthy and influential people who once had proudly called Ilmoure their home. That those plaques tended to be affixed to the benches and picnic tables their money had bought appeared to be mere coincidence. If Ilmoure had a greater need for electric street lamps and museums, Iris was sure the plaques would be attached to those instead. With the way things were, she doubted that would ever be a consideration.

A spot slightly ahead on the path where thin rays of sunlight filtered through the leaves drew her in. Here, one of the older benches with a pompous name to match was facing a gap in the trees; just wide enough to let her glimpse the ocean while hiding away the town below. When Iris pressed her hand to the wood, the almost unnoticeable damp didn't deter her, and she took a seat.

With a weary sigh, she stretched her legs, rested her arms on the back of the bench and watched the mesmerising rise and fall of the waves in the distance. Once, a fishing boat appeared, making its slow way across the bay and out onto the open ocean until it disappeared behind one of the barren little islands dotting the coast. Iris found herself idly wishing whoever was steering it good luck. They certainly needed it. Where other towns like it had found a new fortune in maritime ventures, Ilmoure was adamantly refusing to adapt even now. Maybe that was just the kind of people it bred.

Steps on the path behind her startled Iris from her reverie. It was so peaceful out here, she had almost forgotten that she wasn't on private property. Now, she turned to find someone approaching from the other direction. Instead of walking past, the man disappointed her by coming to a stop near the bench.

"Good day, miss. Would you mind terribly if I joined you in this beautiful spot?"

Iris eyed him warily. Maybe it was the years spent in a city where strangers habitually ignored one's personal space, but something seemed a little off. Like he was just a little too eager to join her.

Or perhaps it was her nerves, and the fact that he clearly wasn't from around here. She'd certainly never seen him before. He looked a good ten years older than she was, with traces of grey along his hairline. In contrast, the kohl around his green eyes and the touch of colour in his cheeks accentuated his most striking features. Attractive enough, Iris mused, if one was fond of men as a concept.

"I suppose not," she finally said. "I don't own the bench."

He gave her a nod and a narrow smile and sat at the end of the bench. At least he had enough manners to keep his distance.

"Are you enjoying the weather?" He leaned back, looking out over the ocean. "You picked a good day to visit. Usually, we get more rain this time of year."

She didn't bother telling him that she knew that. Her lack of answer didn't deter him.

"Are you here on business?"

After a few seconds of silence, Iris accepted that he did indeed expect an answer from her. Maybe then he would shut up.

"You could call it that."

He nodded again. "It's good to take a break from that." The way he looked at her, all sideways and narrow, put her on edge. "Say, have you been about the town yet?"

"A little."

The way she couldn't tell if his smile was sincere bothered her more than it should.

"Marvellous. How do you like it?" More of his teeth showed. "I admit that Ilmoure might look a little dreary at a glance. Truth be told, I only moved here as a favour to an old friend, but the town does have a way of growing you, I think."

Iris shrugged. "I prefer Durham."

"Durham!" Now that smile reached his eyes, which made the other one all the more unsettling. "A woman of culture." He made a sweeping gesture that seemed to encompass everything and nothing. "It's a rather stark difference, wouldn't you say?"

Iris couldn't help but laugh. "That's a bit of an understatement."

"Is that so." The gleam faded from his eyes again. "Anything in particular catch your eye?"

"I don't think so?" She withstood the urge to get up and run, for the moment at least. "Why? Should it?"

His gaze flickered oddly from side to side. "I was rather hoping you could enlighten me, miss. I find that some things are... more obvious to an outside eye."

Iris inched a little sideways. "I don't think I can help you with that."

"Are you sure?" He moved up by precisely the distance she had just gained. "I'm sure there is something about our little town that stands out to you."

Right now, what stood out to her was how alone they were. How far away from everything. Iris swallowed the knot in her throat and stood.

"I'm afraid you're talking to the wrong person." She rounded the bench and stepped back on the path. "Good day. Enjoy your walk."

Only when she'd reached the next bend in the path did she look back. He was watching her, but hadn't left the bench. When he noticed her looking, he quickly turned his head away. Iris turned back around and hurried on.

Great. Fantastic. Not even out here was she guaranteed peace and quiet anymore. Like the whole town and the land it sat on were conspiring against her.

She already could not wait to return home.

IV

I ris made it back to the family home with time to spare, which did not keep the maid from levelling a rather sullen look at her when she opened the door. With a smile that was only slightly nervous, Iris hurried past her, insisting that she could find her own room just fine, thank you.

She took the half hour she had left to wash up, straighten out her hair a little, and change into a fresh shirt. The other one, she left on a clothes hanger for the maid to do with as she saw fit. As ready as she would ever be, Iris returned downstairs for her first family dinner in a long, long time.

She found the dining room all set up but still empty, which gave her another blessed minute to collect her thoughts. The meeting in the afternoon should have given her an idea of what to expect. Instead, it had thrown all of her assumptions overboard, with the way it had felt like she'd left only yesterday. At the same time, they'd made it seem like everything that had transpired before she'd moved to Durham was ancient history, no need to bother with bringing it up anymore. Had she been forgiven? Had *she* forgiven? Try as she might, she could not tell.

It was almost a relief when the door opened again, and in walked her parents. Her mother with the same perfectly smooth and polite expression she'd had the whole time. Her father with a smile that was as wide and bright as Iris remembered, and it made her heart ache.

"Iris!" Anthony Grey crossed the room with a few long strides. "It's so good to see you."

He laid his hands on her shoulders. For a strangely timeless moment, Iris had to resist the urge to slip under her father's grasp and pull him into a hug, like she had done so many times as a girl. Instead, she fixed her expression into a smile, and this time, she barely had to force it. "It really is."

He let go of her and took a step back. "Look at you. You seem to be doing well for yourself." He looked her up and down. Iris couldn't tell if he found what he was looking for before he gestured at the table. "Come on now, sit!" He was the first to do so. "I'm sure we have a lot to talk about."

Iris took a seat, too. "I think so."

It felt a little odd, to see him so carefree. See her mother so calm, and her sister... She glanced at Laura. Laura seemed to be barely present at all, eyes fixed on the table and hands hidden in her lap.

In the span of a few moments, Iris' mood tilted in the strangest way. Wasn't she here for a funeral? Why was everyone acting like she was on a vacation instead?

Was this for her benefit, or Laura's?

The quiet while the maid served the soup felt just a little tense to Iris, while nobody else seemed to be all that bothered by it. Indeed, when the maid had left the room again, her father resumed talking like nothing was wrong at all.

"How is life in Durham treating you?" Anthony Grey studied first the soup in front of him, then his daughter.

Iris wasn't sure which received the harsher judgment in his eyes. "Are you not fed up with it yet?"

"I don't expect to be any time soon," Iris replied. "I have steady employment and a place of my own. It's quite comfortable."

"Employment." He said it like it was unexpected, not a necessity after she had been cut off from all the help Laura had received at her age. "It pays well, I expect?"

"I can afford all I need."

"All you need, eh?" He raised his chin. "And here I thought I raised my daughters to expect only the best."

Iris tried to ignore the turmoil in her stomach. "I write, too." She refused to look at her mother. "I have several paid publications."

"Do you, now?"

The surprise in his words stung, but it was tempered by the small nod right after.

"Not bad, dear. Not bad at all." He took his spoon and began eating. "You're making your way in the world, it seems."

"I'm trying," Iris murmured, wondering if anyone had even heard her as silence fell once more while they ate. At least the soup was good.

"Now, work can't be the only thing you have in Durham, can it." Her father put down his spoon with an indulgent, if slightly tense, little smile. "Have you made friends at university?"

"I have." Iris swallowed the last of her soup with a tight throat. "I'm still in touch with some of them." She gripped the edge of the napkin to hide her trembling hands. What was *wrong* with her? "Emily got me the position I have now. An uncle of hers owns the shop."

"How nice of her." A brief flicker of his eyes, barely noticeable. "What is he selling?"

"Books." Iris managed a tiny smile. "It seemed appropriate."

"Books!" Her father's laughter was startling. "Oh, that is fitting indeed, isn't it, Katherine?"

Her mother's smile was measured with pinpoint precision. "It truly is. We shouldn't have expected anything else."

Her father nodded like that hadn't been a slight. "Well, it would seem natural for our daughter to take part in a business."

Iris stared at her empty plate. "I'm an employee, it's not like I manage the place."

He made a dismissive sound. "And who is to say you won't manage a business one day?"

Well, it wasn't what she was aiming for, but Iris decided not to disappoint him so soon. Instead, she nodded silently and suppressed the urge to hug Olivia when she came back to carry away the plates and serve the next course. It gave her a few moments to work up the courage to not-so-subtly change the subject once they were alone again.

"Ilmoure has changed a lot." She stared at the perfectly cooked fish on her plate, served with just the right amount of a creamy sauce. "How are things around here?"

"Oh, don't worry too much about the looks." Her father began cutting his fish with surgical precision. "We're doing just fine."

"Really?" Iris glanced up, but nobody was looking at her. "It all looked so..." She fumbled for a better word and failed. "Closed."

"There have been some changes," her father said lightly, "but not everyone seems to be cut out for this kind of place anymore." He inclined his head. "The allure of the big city, I'm sure you understand."

Iris almost choked on her food. "Yes? I... suppose."

The last time they had spoken, he had been shouting about how it was a disgrace to move away. How a place like Durham could never offer her what Ilmoure had – even though he had failed to provide a single example of what that was. And Iris had shouted back, and things had gotten louder, until she'd taken her bags and left, and then she had refused to speak to him the one time he had called the faculty office. Two lines in a letter, and a single one in return, had been all they had exchanged since then.

And now he was *joking* about it. Like none of it mattered.

Like the past six years had been just so *funny*.

Iris' grip around the cutlery became so hard as to be painful. She forced herself to let go with a slow, measured exhale. He was trying. Maybe that was it. Maybe this was to be a fresh start, and it was all behind them, and she wasn't being fair.

So she took a steadying breath, plastered a smile onto her face, and tried, too. "So, what is there to do around town these days?"

She hadn't felt this tired after a dinner since the first time she'd gone with Mr. Williams to meet a client for his antique side venture. That man had talked and talked and talked and worn them both out so thoroughly that Mr. Williams hadn't even mentioned her sour attitude the next day. Tonight, Iris felt like she was back in that crowded restaurant again, listening to entirely too much information about all those beautiful train routes in Europe and how nice the Alps were in spring, waiting for a single, solitary thing to lead them back to the business transaction they were meant to conduct. She nodded and smiled and made the occasional comment and non-committal noise until, to her endless relief, the empty dessert bowls were replaced with coffee and brandy. At that point, it wasn't long until Laura excused herself, which in turn signalled the end of the evening for everyone. Iris wanted to squeeze her sister until she ran out of air, but wisely refrained. Instead, she wished everybody a good night and retreated to her own room, feeling thoroughly wrung out.

If every day would be like this, she'd need some more time off to recover before she put in that overtime at the store.

V

I ris slept like the dead until the early morning, when she woke up at precisely the same time she always did – and a good hour early for breakfast. So for once, she took advantage of having an abundance of time in the morning. She thoroughly enjoyed the reliable hot water and made sure she looked as presentable as she could manage before she got dressed and made her way downstairs.

In the family room, she browsed the shelf that held the books that hadn't been purchased to impress visitors and business partners. The ones with deadly intrigue and salacious secrets, that her mother had done her best to hide from her, and failed miserably by the time Iris turned twelve.

Now, those books served as an entertaining distraction before a rather subdued breakfast. Once again, Laura joined them for that, albeit still so quiet as to barely count as present.

"Is Daniel not home at the moment?"

Her father didn't reply. Her mother shared a look with Laura, who then twisted her expression into an approximation of a smile.

"He's out of town for work," she said. "I'm afraid he won't be back for some time, so I moved back home for company until then."

"Oh." Iris reached for another slice of toast and the jam jar to buy herself a moment. "Will he not be there... this afternoon?"

It had to be obvious what she meant, yet Laura's smile did not falter. "Unfortunately not. He just couldn't make the time."

Iris bit her tongue to keep an unfavourable comment to herself. What kind of husband and father couldn't just ditch his work for his own child's funeral?

"A shame," she eventually choked out. "I suppose sometimes it just doesn't work out."

Whether her question had stirred up hurt or other, more complicated feelings, Iris couldn't tell – they finished the meal in silence. After, they got ready to head out to church, which for Iris largely meant sitting in the family room waiting for everyone else to come back down. To pass the time, she paced along the walls, the shelves and display cases. They held largely the same things she remembered. The little figurines, the more expensive portraits, the old gramophone that she'd only ever seen in use for the most special occasions. The last time for Laura's engagement party.

Iris stood before the row of pictures on the wall. Daniel Alden smiled serenely out of the frame, as if he wasn't letting down his wife right this second. She looked left and right, but found no other pictures of him. In fact, there were no family pictures at all beyond the older ones, from before she had left. Not a sign of Daniel, or indeed Matthew.

"Oh."

Iris traced one of the darker spots. Was that why? The most generous explanation was that it hurt Laura too much. The less generous interpretation might be that they treated Matthew as out of sight, out of mind.

It certainly wouldn't seem out of line with how strangely absent he had been from the conversation since she had arrived, despite being the reason she was here.

She flinched away from the pictures, startled from her less than charitable thoughts, when someone knocked on the door and Olivia the maid stuck her head inside.

"Mr. and Mrs. Grey and Mrs. Alden are leaving now."

Iris quickly tried to compose herself. "Thank you. I'll be right there."

When she joined them downstairs, she felt decidedly out of place. They were in the expected mourning attire, while Iris herself had settled for the darkest suit she owned, which had very obviously not been bought for the occasion. She brushed down the front of her coat and tried to ignore what her nervous mind insisted was irreversible judgement in their eyes.

"I'm ready."

Her father looked her up and down, and opted for a solemn nod in return. "Let's not keep Father Melville waiting."

The walk to the graveyard was short and quiet until they reached the gates and went down the path leading to the church in the centre of the area. The church was one of the oldest buildings in Ilmoure, and these days, it looked like it, too. Where the facade had been white and shiny in Iris' memory, now it was grey, with several feet of ivy climbing up the shallow slope from the messy lawn around. The bells were silent, too, and Iris couldn't help but wonder if they'd broken with no money to replace them, or been sold to maintain the rest of the building. To add a lock to the front door, the dull steel out of place against the dark oak, and replace one of the stained-glass windows with a plain one. It looked at least a century too new among the rest.

They didn't enter. Instead, her father led them around and behind the church. A small crowd was waiting among the stately old grave markers of marble and granite, a throng of people clad in black and grey and dark blue. Their approach drew looks both curious and oddly offended. Iris resisted the urge to pull on her cuffs and puff out her chest. Her state of dress was suitable. That she was not as old-fashioned as her sister was nobody's business.

When they had passed through the crowd, Iris trailing just a little behind, she expected her parents to flank Laura, sheltering her like they always had. Instead, when her sister stopped, they left a space between them, standing side by side like a pair of statues, their faces just as motionless. Leaving the grieving mother at the front of the crowd, closest to the man in a black robe standing at the head of an open grave. The coffin in front of him, suspended on thick ropes, looked horrifically small. A stark reminder how little time Matthew had spent on this earth. How little time Iris had spent trying to get to know her nephew.

With a fog in her mind and a weight on her chest, she ignored the looks all around and stood next to Laura. She left just enough space between them to let her decide if she wanted to acknowledge her little sister right now.

The breaths between were cold. Slow and agonising as Iris waited. Wondered if what had been between them when they were children was now broken for good.

Laura reached out. "Iris."

A lump in her throat, Iris reached back, across the tiny gap. Laura's fingers closed briefly, firmly despite the tremors. Just for a moment before Laura let go again, tucked her hands into the folds of her dress under her belly, and looked straight ahead at her son's coffin.

Silence fell as if on cue, and the robed man stepped forward, startling Iris. One last furtive glance around, and she saw that the crowd had closed in, leaving no gap to the outside to let anyone else into the circle of mourners.

The preacher, who had to be Father Melville, cleared his throat. Bony fingers clutched a heavy, leather-bound book as he scanned the crowd, a finger pinned between the yellowed pages. Someone coughed, and he scowled. He wrapped his hands around the book, closing it all the way, and looked ahead.

"We have gathered here today to mourn young Matthew Alden. When a child is taken from his parents…"

He fell into a familiar monotone, reciting familiar phrases and making familiar gestures. Soon enough, Iris had to look away, tears pricking her eyes despite herself. For her sister, her nephew, and what could have been. She did her best to blink them away. If anyone had a right to cry, it was Laura – and her face was as dry and still as those of the statues around them.

The speech was short, and instead of a prayer, the preacher ended with a minute of silence that felt oddly pointed. Once again, his gaze scanned the crowd before he took a step back and motioned for two men in drab clothes and dark caps to lower the coffin. They did so quietly and quickly, so much so that it almost surprised Iris when they stepped back and the preacher made another gesture above the open grave, this time less familiar.

"May he find peace in eternity."

The crowd repeated it, a sombre mumble at Iris' back. Laura's voice next to her was shaky. From the corner of her eye, Iris saw her lean forward ever so slightly, until her father caught her arm. A look passed between them, and Laura turned away from her son's grave.

They stood as if they were a proper family again, next to each other a few feet away from the headstone, as the crowd filed past them. 'I'm sorry', 'my condolences', and 'deepest sympathies' washed over them like rain. Laura accepted each one with a nod, and their father expressed thanks on her behalf. Towards the end, a woman Laura's age lingered. They had gone to school together, and that was all Iris remembered. The woman took both of Laura's hands in hers with a smile.

"It will get easier."

Laura nodded again – this time smiling, too. "Thank you."

Iris abruptly turned her head. A question on her tongue, she tried to catch Laura's eye. Instead, motion behind her sister distracted her. Her father's eyes locking with hers. The subtle shake of his head made the words die on her tongue.

Fingers toying with a loose thread at the edge of her sleeve, Iris looked ahead again. She might have misheard – or misinterpreted. Perhaps Laura and that woman were closer friends than she remembered. A shared pain might be a comfort, if there was any sort of comfort to be found in this.

Laura went back to her nods and their father kept saying his thanks until the last one had walked past them. Finally, Father Melville took his turn, standing before Laura and smiling like an indulgent uncle.

"You bear a heavy burden, child."

He laid a hand on her shoulder. For the first time, Laura seemed less than serene. It was brief, just a twitch, but Iris didn't miss it. Still, Laura returned that smile.

"Be assured that this trial will not be in vain." The preacher let go and bent his head towards their parents. "May you walk the path to eternity with your head held high."

Then he, too, turned and walked away, leaving them alone by the open grave. The only others left were the two men who were leaning on shovels and did very much look like they wanted them gone sooner rather than later.

Her mother, it seemed, noticed, too.

"We should leave." She laid a hand on Laura's shoulder, where the preacher had. This time, Laura didn't move. "It will be over soon."

They turned around and walked away without so much as another look. Iris lingered, glancing at the church. No service at all. What had been the point of having a priest conduct the funeral, then?

Before she followed, Iris cast one last look at the grave. The headstone with the name and the heartbreaking dates. Not even a flower on it. She looked around, but there was nothing but trampled grass and weeds.

"Iris." Her father beckoned her. "We mustn't be late, now."

Then he, too, left without another word.

Under the watchful eyes of the graveyard keepers, Iris knelt and plucked a few unscathed daisies from the grass behind another grave marker. Tied them together with the stem of another, and laid them on the headstone. She ignored the sharp exhale and the stab of metal into dirt behind her as she hurried to follow her father.

At the funeral, Iris' focus had been on the preacher, and she had been able to ignore the looks aimed at her back. At the wake, with everyone crowding into the salon on Folsom Street, she didn't have that luxury. At least here, most people did not linger long enough to spare her more than a distrustful glance or two.

Once again, Laura was accepting expressions of sympathy, this time seated in an armchair, hands folded on her belly. The disconnect was jarring, and Iris had some difficulty looking at her like this. The way she acted, one could almost think she was taking congratulations on a child to be born, not condolences for one just buried. It wasn't like the sister Iris had known. Guilt twisting her stomach, she turned away. She herself had changed so much since that day. How was she expecting Laura to still be the same? Or anyone?

She drifted away for a moment, taking her glass into a corner of the room where she pretended to appreciate the porcelain figurines in a display case. Dancers, young women with flower baskets, a couple leaning close to each other, like they were trading secrets. Among the figurines, more modern artwork was displayed. Delicate, abstract forms of glass, and an esoteric-looking symbol of polished gold that would not have looked out of place in a séance at one of Durham's more eccentric salons. As strange as Iris had found those the few times Emily had insisted they go together, even that would have been preferable to this abject misery.

Proper manners dictated that she stay with her family. She tried. Every time someone new came over, their gaze lingered on Laura. Acknowledged her parents. Skipped her like she wasn't even there.

Well. That was better than the looks. Some remembered her, no doubt, and the way she had left Ilmoure, too. They made it very clear that they approved of it about as much as her parents had. Although unlike her parents, they very much did not act in the spirit of forgive and forget. Iris definitely preferred the ones who didn't even know who she was

What she was supposed to make of the other ones, she wasn't sure at all. She remembered a few of them. They did everything the others did. They talked at Laura, accepted thank yous from their parents, and then looked at Iris with those odd expressions and little smiles and 'welcome homes' and 'good to see you backs'. Iris wanted to dispute them every time they raked across her skin. It would have been tiresome, not to mention spectacularly rude for the occasion, so Iris bit her tongue, made non-committal noises, and hoped it all would indeed be over soon.

"Mrs. Alden. I am so sorry for your loss."

The voice startled Iris out of a reverie. It took her several moments to understand why this one and not the others. When she looked up from her spot on the floor, she found the man from the forest path standing in front of Laura. She couldn't help but notice that his face was plain now.

"Matthew was such a bright student," the man continued. "It is a shame he took ill so young."

Laura's narrow, steady smile never faltered, but tiny creases appeared around her eyes. Their father leaned in, taking the man's hand to shake it.

"Thank you, Mr. Mason, we appreciate your sympathy."

"Naturally." Mr. Mason nodded solemnly. His gaze flickered to Iris. "It's quite tragic, having to see so many of my students go in such a short time."

"Sometimes, fate strikes where we least expect it," Anthony Grey said pointedly. "We can't do anything but accept it with grace."

Mr. Mason eyed him with a strangely hard expression. "If I may take this moment, Mr. Grey. I have former colleagues who might quite like to take a look at these cases. Perhaps there is a manner of prevention to be found, or even a-"

"We have consulted with experts," her father said curtly. "There is nothing to be done."

"With all due respect, I don't think we should give up so easily," Mr. Mason argued, much less gently than before. "If we could find the cause of this ailment-"

"Mr. Mason." The way her father raised his voice turned more than a few heads, and the volume of the conversation around changed in an instant. "We appreciate your concern, but this is, quite frankly, nothing you should be worrying about."

"It is quite difficult not to worry about my students," Mr. Mason replied, his tone clipped. "Seeing how they keep leaving the way they do."

"I understand." Heat in her father's voice, now. "I still must insist that this is none of your business."

For a moment, it looked like the man wanted to argue right back, but much to Iris' relief, he didn't get a word out before her father continued.

"I am afraid you must be going now." Anthony Grey's smile could have cut glass. "We would not dare keep you from your weekend, and we have matters to attend to shortly."

A red tint rose into the man's cheeks, but he clenched his jaw and nodded. "Of course. My apologies. I would not keep you from those." He inclined his head at Laura. "Mrs. Alden."

A curious glance at Iris, another silent nod, and then he turned on his heel and left. Iris watched him disappear into the hallway, and when she heard the front door close, she looked at her father, who was glaring after the man with unexpected disdain. Iris had to convince herself to speak.

"Who was that?"

Anthony Grey exhaled, long and deliberate. When he replied, his voice was perfectly even. "He has the misfortune of being Miss Alito's replacement at the school. Richard enticed him to take the position after quite a few weeks, and I wish he had kept looking for longer." He sighed deeply. "Don't concern yourself with him."

"Clara is gone? Why did she leave?"

"We would all like to know that," her mother replied curtly. "One morning, she simply did not come to class."

It sounded rather final, and both her and her father returned their attention to the proceedings once again. Iris swallowed any questions she might have liked to ask; she was unlikely to receive any answers, it seemed.

Whether or not there really was anything else waiting to be done in the afternoon, the interaction had inadvertently signalled an end to the wake. People emptied their glasses, wished them farewell, and filed out the door alone and in pairs and small groups. In the end, only the four of them were left, as well as the maid, who swiftly left them to their own devices. When her footfalls disappeared down the hall, Iris finally felt like she could breathe again.

"Iris."

Once again, it was Laura who spoke so softly. This time, she had approached her, with that same narrow smile she had worn throughout the wake.

"Thank you for coming."

Bewildered, Iris nodded silently before she found her voice again. "Of course I came."

The smile never faltered. "I know. I'm still glad to see you."

And with that, she turned and walked away, leaving Iris feeling a little dizzy and breathless and wondering if Laura was playing a rather lengthy joke on her.

"Don't be too harsh on her."

The hand on her shoulder was her mother's. Where it had looked soothing with Laura, Iris felt like she was about to have a set of claws buried in her flesh.

"She is exhausted. This has been difficult for her."

Has it? Iris swallowed that question. It wasn't like she got to judge anyone for keeping an unhealthy amount of emotions hidden away. Instead, she redirected her confusion elsewhere.

"She shouldn't have been alone. Daniel should have been here."

Her mother's fingertips pressed down, and her smile seemed to grow some teeth. "He was unable to leave his responsibilities."

Iris stepped sideways, shaking off her mother's hand and pretending to look out the window. "His son died."

Katherine's tone gained an edge. "It couldn't be helped."

Iris looked back at her mother. "I made it work."

"So you did." Her father joined them. "We all appreciate it."

Iris wasn't quite so sure about that. A stubborn reply died on her tongue when she remembered the morning. "I should go, too." She glanced at the door. "I'm expecting a telegram, and the post office closes early today."

"Of course." Her father nodded slowly. A thin smile spread on his face. "Do make sure you're home in time for dinner, will you?"

"I will," Iris muttered, before she plastered a smile of her own onto his face. "I'll be seeing you later."

VI

T he telegram was waiting for her when she got to the post office. Much to Iris' relief, Mr. Williams did not mind her extending her stay. She would indeed be working the coming holidays in full, at her usual hourly pay. Iris tried not to be too resentful about it.

At least she still had a job to return to.

With that out of the way, Iris found herself once again with nothing to do. Returning to the house seemed... unpleasant right now. She ambled down the street, hands in her pockets. It was a little too overcast for comfort, so she didn't turn towards the trails outside of town. Instead, she passed by the schoolhouse and made her way to the library. Maybe rifling through the shelves would help take her mind off of things until she inevitably had to face yet another family dinner.

She climbed the stairs and entered the building through the open front door into a dimly lit foyer. Nothing moved inside. The front desk was empty. The whole building felt like it was. Durham University's library felt like a beehive most days. This place was a dried-up wasps' nest in the attic of an empty house. It almost turned her right back around. The only reason she didn't was the idea of spending the entire afternoon either cooped up in her room, or worse, making conversation with her mother again.

Stairs led up to the next floor, and three open doors marked with brass signs invited her to see if anything new had made its way onto the shelves since she'd last been here. Iris' shoes clicked on the black and white diamond pattern of the floor as she walked past the desk and into the largest of the rooms. Down here, old novelists leaned into each other for comfort, with few books standing out with colourful backs and bold script. The rest of the room was a pattern of faded reds, blues, greens, browns, the stamped titles getting progressively harder to read. Iris trailed her fingers along this one and that one, reading titles at an angle or simply feeling the groves where the foil had worn off on some. A few, she stopped to pull out, studying the front matter, but none of them convinced her they were worth checking out.

The sharp, rhythmic clicking of heels on the floor tugged at her attention. A feeling of familiarity washed over her that she couldn't pinpoint. She'd barely put the book back when someone addressed her from much too close by.

"Can I help you?"

"Maybe." Iris turned around. "I was wondering if you still had my... file..." The words fell to the ground like wilted petals. "Cat."

"We keep- Iris?"

She was as stunned as Iris was, but recovered much more quickly. The set of her mouth became firm, and a frown shadowed her brown eyes as she looked Iris up and down, from the shoes to the suit and the hair cut to just above her shoulders. Unbidden, Iris wondered if Cat liked it. Considering how much of a change it was.

Of course, it didn't seem to matter one bit.

"What are you doing here?"

Iris' mouth went dry. "Trying to borrow a book."

"No." Cat's voice could have cut steel. "What are you doing *here?*"

It was inordinately difficult to stay where she was and reply like she didn't desperately want to turn tail and run. "I'm here for the funeral. My mother asked me to attend."

"Your mother."

Breathe. Why was it so hard to keep breathing. "Is that so hard to believe?"

"The last time you two spoke to each other, I could hear the screaming from outside." Cat's nostrils flared. "Would you like me to tell you what she said to you? Because I remember that day incredibly well."

Iris tried to swallow the bone in her throat, to no avail. "Cat, I'm-"

"It's *Cateleya.*"

A deep breath. Trying not to be too hurt, because she probably deserved this. "Cateleya. Apologies. That was presumptuous."

Cateleya studied her for an uncomfortable amount of time. Whatever judgement she came to at the end, it manifested in a tiny sigh and an almost imperceptible slump of her shoulders.

"Quit being so formal, it doesn't suit you." Cateleya's features softened unexpectedly. "I shouldn't have snapped. I just didn't expect to see you here."

Or ever again, it seemed. Iris nodded weakly.

"I didn't plan on being back, if I'm being honest. But I couldn't ignore the... invite."

She almost winced at her own words. What a crass way to phrase it. Then again, the way it had reached her, it had seemed more like a summons, so why should she care.

To her surprise, Cateleya chuckled. "If your mother hasn't changed, I'm sure you couldn't." Once again, she was too quiet for a bit. "So. Durham. I suppose it's a big change to be back in Ilmoure."

"You could say that."

Only now did Iris feel like she could allow herself to really *look at* Cateleya. She'd changed since last time, of course she had. But so much was still the same that it almost hurt. The way she held her head so high. How neat she wore her hair, the dark braid twisting tightly at the back of her head. How impeccable her clothes looked over-

Oh. That certainly was a rather *big change*.

Iris quickly tore her eyes away from the small bump in Cateleya's midsection.

"It's..." Why was her throat so dry? She tried again. "It's been a while since I've been anywhere so... tranquil."

"Tranquil." The way Cateleya's lips curled, Iris almost wanted to believe she was fighting a smile. "There's the writer."

Iris huffed out a laugh. "I thought calling it boring would have been rude."

Cateleya shrugged. "It would have been honest."

And yet you stayed.

She kept that to herself. The one letter she'd dared to send had never received an answer. Not to her apology, and not to her offer to have Cateleya move in, to do this together. After all this time, maybe she'd simply forgotten – or she had never cared in the first place.

"How are things here?" Iris looked around at the empty room, to avoid looking at Cateleya more than anything else. So she wouldn't have to ask... "It doesn't look like much has changed."

"I suppose that depends on who you're asking," Cateleya replied. "The way I've heard it, your father's business has been rather thriving."

"I'm not sure," Iris admitted. "I didn't ask. It felt a little misplaced, considering the circumstances."

Not that it seemed to matter much to anyone else, Iris mused. Which was still all kinds of odd. Did they *expect* her to ask? Was this a test, of her willingness to be accepted back into the fold? Was that why everything was feeling so... superficial? Was she failing already?

"I should have said." Cateleya sounded strangely gentle now. "I'm really sorry about Matthew."

Iris nodded weakly. "Thank you." Her cheeks felt hot as she squeezed the next words out. "I wish I'd gotten to know him better."

"I understand." Cateleya wrapped her arms around herself. "I'm glad you came. It's got to be so difficult for Laura, so shortly after Rose."

Iris bit her tongue, trying not to argue, because who was she to judge? "I suppose it..."

She trailed off when she caught up and tripped over those words. Looked at Cateleya, suddenly on guard.

"What do you mean, after Rose?"

Cateleya seemed taken aback. "What?"

Iris worked her jaw as a few things fell into place. "Who is Rose?" She made a vague gesture. "Was Laura close to someone?"

Was *that* why Daniel was out of town for his own son's funeral? And why Laura was living at the family home again? It seemed implausible, but not impossible. Her parents had always cared about appearances. Maybe this was the price to keep the marriage alive and spare the family from public humiliation.

It certainly would explain a lot of the awkwardness around... everything.

"I... would assume so?" Cateleya looked at her cautiously. "Do you not know about Rose?"

Iris sneered. "I have not exactly been kept in the loop when it comes to Laura's private *affairs*."

"Her affairs?" Cateleya seemed startled. Even more so when understanding crossed her face. "Iris, this is not... Rose was Laura's daughter."

Head suddenly rather empty, Iris stared at her. "Excuse me?"

"Her daughter," Cateleya repeated gently. "Your niece."

"I don't have a niece."

It was obvious. It *sounded* obvious, too, but somehow, Cateleya didn't seem to care. She just kept staring, and the look blooming on her face was all kinds of unsettling.

"Did they never tell you?"

Iris was irrationally proud of herself for not looking away this time. "Tell me what, exactly?"

She hated that look of pity on Cateleya's face.

"Laura had a daughter," Cateleya said gently. "The year after you left. That was Rose. She died last year."

"She died."

Iris leaned against the shelf, as if that would help somehow. Maybe it did. Her knees felt weak, like she should perhaps have a little sit-down, but she felt rooted in place. Her hand gripped the edge of the shelf behind her until it hurt.

"I had a niece, and she died."

Cateleya nodded, once. She didn't say anything. Simply allowed Iris to sort through those words – and what they meant, right here, right now.

"Nobody ever told me." She took a shaky breath, and it was all she could do not to let it become a sob. "Why didn't they tell me?"

It didn't make sense. They had told her about Matthew, when he died and they wanted her to be there. If there had been another child, even if Laura hadn't thought or bothered to write to her, if she hadn't cared enough to let her know, which wasn't undeserved...

Why had nobody mentioned anything when she had arrived? Why hadn't a single person said a single thing? Surely, if they had expected her to stay in the house, she would have seen or found *something*, and then what? Hope she wouldn't ask questions?

"Iris?"

Where she'd been brusque before, now Cateleya sounded so soft and gentle, like she'd always been unless some steel was needed. She was close, but didn't touch – whether or not Iris wanted her to, she wasn't sure herself.

"I'm all right." In the broadest sense, anyway. "I'm..." Iris shook her head and stood up straight, back rigid and her hand now a fist at her side. "I need to... think." She briefly caught Cateleya's gaze again before she couldn't bear it and looked away. "Thank you for telling me."

With that, she brushed past Cateleya and stalked out of the room. Through the foyer and down the stairs, and through the streets without really knowing where she was going. Just that she couldn't go home, not yet.

Maybe she shouldn't have gone back in the first place.

It just didn't make any sense. She knew about Matthew. And she had inquired about the family, the few times she'd written home. Surely that included any other children Laura might have had while Iris had been gone?

Someone should have discussed it, now that she was here. Especially considering the occasion. Iris bit her lip. Quite how such a conversation should have gone, she couldn't imagine. But something should have been said, shouldn't it? At the very least, so Iris did not embarrass herself, or the family.

She trudged ahead along the edge of town, brooding on all the possible reasons why she hadn't been told. All that she managed to come back to was that either Iris' presence was considered so unimportant that nobody had thought of it – or her niece was.

Iris wasn't entirely sure which idea felt worse to her, which made her feel horribly selfish, and she quickly shook her head to rid herself of the though. It was only marginally successful.

When she reached the long wall around the churchyard, Iris was surprised how far she'd gotten. Or how long she'd been in thought. She wasn't sure which it was, and she couldn't be bothered to check. Still, now that she was here...

She entered the graveyard through the gate, walking into an eerily empty and silent area. For how many dead the town had, few people seemed to bother remembering them. Maybe that was it. Maybe Ilmoure had just made a habit out of forgetting its deceased while she hadn't been looking.

It might have seemed that way to an outsider, Iris mused as she made her way between the headstones and the few scattered monuments. She hadn't noticed it earlier, but now it felt unavoidable. Not a single wreath, no bouquets, not even a bundle of flowers picked from the side of the gravel paths winding between the resting places of Ilmoure's ancestors.

Eventually, she reached Matthew's grave. The dirt mound sat there, fresh and bare and ready to fade into the ground. A few days, maybe a good, strong rain, and it would be gone. The daisies had fallen off the headstone, wilting into the fresh soil. Hands in her pockets, Iris stood there for a silent minute of respect, now that nobody was bothering her to leave. She searched for anything else, some fond memories to make it feel more sincere, but there was so little. Nothing that made her feel like she deserved to be here. Iris made a hasty turn and walked away, along the rows of newer headstones, searching.

Row after row, she checked for the name, and each time, she came up with nothing. With a deepening frown, she kept walking, checking between the older headstones now. Even finding others with familiar names, more Greys and Aldens and a few McNamaras from her mother's side. But no Rose Alden. No child named Rose who had died in the last year. No Rose at all besides one who had passed away long before Iris had been born, buried at the edge of the last row where her headstone was nearly unreadable from all the moss.

Iris stood by it, looking back out over the graveyard, her hurt fading into the background, replaced by more confusion. If there had been a Rose Alden, why wasn't she here? Why wasn't she laid to rest next to her brother?

By the church, someone moved. At first, Iris assumed another mourner. Then she noticed the robes. Quickly, she made her way between the headstones.

"Father!"

When he heard her call out so close, he froze for a moment, hand on the handle of the church door and holding a large key. He turned it with force as his head snapped up. "Yes?"

"I'm sorry." Iris stopped a few feet away. "I didn't mean to intrude." She glanced over her shoulder, back at the dirt mound in the distance. "You wouldn't happen to know who has been buried here in the past year or so?"

The preacher pocketed the key and eyed her warily. "Perhaps."

"I'm looking for Rose Alden." Iris tried to sound even. Curious, but not too much. "She died some time last year, around... four years old?"

He stared at her for too long. "You must be mistaken, child. There is no Rose Alden buried here."

"What?"

"If she was that young, I would remember." He inclined his head. "There is no-one by that name buried in this churchyard."

"But..." That didn't sound right. Why wouldn't she be? "She should be here."

"Is that so." He sounded just like her father. "Are you quite certain that you have the right name to look for?"

Iris paused. Was she? All she had was Cateleya's word. "Maybe I need to make sure." She nodded absently. "Thank you for your time, father."

"Any time, child."

Iris left him behind, but the feeling of eyes on her back remained. By the gate, she looked back; he was still standing by the door, unmoving. Iris quickly turned away and left.

More questions, and Iris wasn't sure if she wanted to know the answers. There had to be an explanation. Maybe they simply hadn't known how to have that conversation. Maybe Laura refused to be reminded of another tragic loss. Maybe there had been a misunderstanding, some way Cateleya had misinterpreted things, and there had never been a Rose Alden at all.

Whatever the case, she wouldn't find this explanation out here. Best to calm herself, think it all over, and perhaps figure out a way to phrase this most delicate of questions without starting yet another bout of family drama. That was the last thing anybody needed right now.

VII

After more aimless meandering through Ilmoure's streets, underneath an ever-growing layer of clouds, Iris barely made it home in time to make herself presentable for dinner. It was a quiet, awkward affair. Laura didn't say a single word, which Iris didn't blame her for. The rest of them spread out the most vapid, superficial conversation over long pauses and non-committal noises. Leaving half her food untouched, Iris almost laughed in relief when her mother excused herself alongside Laura, allowing her to retreat early as well.

She had tried. Tried to find the most innocuous way to ask, the most opportune time to bring it up, and the courage to do so. She'd failed on all accounts when she finally closed the door to the guest room behind herself. Every time she had *almost* dared to ask, she'd cast another look at Laura, who had now buried two children and would have to raise a third haunted by that spectre, and the words had died on her tongue.

Frustrated, agitated and irritated at herself, Iris tried to busy herself as best she could in an attempt to forget about the whole thing. If they wanted her to know, she reasoned, they would have told her long ago. If they cared enough to bring it up, they would have done so when she had arrived. With an itch at the back of her mind and a knot of anxiety in her stomach, Iris eventually went to bed and tried to will herself to sleep.

The gloom outside had changed into a proper seaside storm when Iris woke up. With the room still pitch black, it couldn't have been too long since she'd finally managed to fall asleep. She turned sideways, squeezing her eyes shut, but now that she was aware of it, the noise scratched her mind with irritating persistence. Where the rain battering the window might have been soothing any other night, now it was like nails on a chalkboard. The wind creaking the old structure of the house made her flinch every time.

Eventually, Iris gave up and groped for the lamp on the bedside table. The switch clicked, and the room stayed dark. Iris turned onto her back again. Delightful.

Now wide awake and with nothing to do, Iris stared into the darkness, and her mind began to wander. Back to the previous day, to the library and Cateleya, and... everything else. It should have all seemed so much more unbelievable now. Like a bad dream. Maybe Cateleya still held a grudge, and rightfully so – although this kind of cruelty, Iris decided, wasn't quite as deserved, and Cateleya had never been prone to it in the first place. If anything, out of the two of them, she'd always been the better person.

So try as she might, she could not convince herself that she'd fallen for a lie, a disgusting joke. And if she ruled this out, if she accepted that Cateleya had told her the truth, or what she perceived as the truth...

She had to make sure. If she could see with her own eyes, if she *knew* that a Rose Alden had lived and died in this town, then she could begin to unravel what that meant – and why she wasn't supposed to know.

But for that, she *had to make sure.*

Iris threw the covers aside and set her feet on the cold floor. Where her slippers were, she didn't quite remember, and it was too dark to see. So she fumbled with the curtains for some semblance of light from outside, still found nothing, and eventually made her way barefoot across the room to the door. She cracked it open and peered outside, straining her ears to listen over the sound of the rain. Nothing moved in the house, and after one last moment of hesitation, Iris slipped outside and made her way down to the family room.

The stairs and the floorboards still creaked exactly where they always had, and the first few times, Iris flinched, freezing where she was, like she, too, was suddenly ten years younger again and sneaking out to meet Cateleya for a moonlight walk. The next few steps, she skipped as quietly as she could, and sighed in relief when she made it down without anybody calling out to her for being up at this forsaken hour.

The family room was slightly brighter, with the curtains never drawn and letting the light from the gas lamps in. It wasn't quite enough to see the pictures, but enough to find an old lamp on the mantle. For decoration or just in case, Iris didn't know, but she was nonetheless relived to find it still functional. She struck a match from the box next to it, lit the flame, and took the lamp over to the wall to get some much needed clarity.

There they all were, frozen in time like nothing had ever happened. Like they were still as happy as they had been at that church picnic, when a photographer had come for some kind of anniversary and taken family pictures for purchase. Iris glanced at the date in the corner. If she remembered that right, it had been one of the last times she'd ever worn a dress. In hindsight, that was when the constant fighting had started.

She moved on quickly, to wedding pictures and a portrait of her parents and one of Laura alone. Another one, the three of them, dated two years ago. Iris paused. Looked at the pictures surrounding it. Just one more to the right, of Laura and their mother. That was it.

No more pictures of Iris, and not a single photograph of either Matthew or Rose.

Iris took a step back, looking up and down the row of photographs once more. The pictures had always had pride of place in the family room. Now, so many were missing, and barely a trace of herself or Laura's husband. And none at all of not just one, but two children who should be here, right next to the rest of the family.

It was almost enough to convince her that she'd been lied to after all. That this Rose wasn't actually an Alden. That she had interfered in Laura's marriage, and that this was the reason her sister was living in the family home again – and Daniel hadn't bothered with the funeral.

Then again, why keep the wedding picture, if the marriage was as good as over? Surely, it wasn't kept in the *family* room for appearances' sake.

Iris leaned against the back of the couch, holding the serene gaze of Laura's latest portrait that was so vacuous it might as well have come with the frame. She'd come here for an answer, and now she had even more questions. This just didn't feel right. Family secrets were for big manor houses and old nobility. They didn't belong into the townhouse where she'd played so much hide and seek growing up that she knew every little nook and cranny.

Or at least, thought she did until a minute ago.

Iris took another tour around the room, peering into every cabinet and looking over every shelf to see if she might have missed something. If the explanation she was so desperately looking for might be hiding in plain sight. It wasn't.

Defeated, exhausted, and head full of more questions than the day before, Iris left the family room and returned upstairs. Again, she tried to be quiet, this time aided by the flickering light of the lamp so she could avoid the creaky spots, especially right by the other bedrooms. Wouldn't want to wake...

Iris startled when she approached Laura's old room. It was still hers, that much she knew – and now the door was open by a good foot, revealing a line of solid darkness.

Frozen in place, Iris listened. Had she woken her up on the way down? Had the door already been open then? Impossible to say. In the dark, she hadn't noticed. Now, she peered into the black but found understandably nothing. So she listened, trying to decide whether she should creep past or attempt to apologise.

Instead, all she heard was silence.

Frowning, Iris closed the distance. Now directly next to the open door, she tried to make out any kind of sound. Breathing, a cough, even a more undignified noise would have calmed her down. All she heard was the rain drumming on the window.

"Laura?"

Her whisper fell to the ground, heavy and unheard. That was unlike Laura. She'd always been the one to complain about even the slightest imaginary noise. Iris pushed open the door and looked inside.

The bed was empty.

"What the hell?"

Throat dry and heart pounding, Iris looked around. The bed was made and Laura's nightgown was folded at the end. Like this was just an ordinary day, except it was the wee hours of the morning and it was storming outside.

"Laura?"

Of course there was no reply, and Iris didn't hold out for one. Instead, she went back into the hall. Went to knock on the bathroom door, but it, too, was empty.

So Iris went downstairs. A late-night snack for a pregnant woman seemed perfectly normal. Maybe it would even put Laura in the mood to talk. Give Iris a chance to get some answers.

The kitchen was quiet and dark. So were the pantry and the salon. With every room, Iris concern shifted, then grew. She still didn't dare call out, but she hurried back upstairs. Marched down the hall and banged on the door at the end of it.

"Father?" She slammed her fist against the wood again. "Mother?"

Nothing. Iris wrenched the knob so hard that it creaked and opened the door herself, response be damned.

"Father? Laura's gone, and I don't know where-"

She abruptly fell silent when the light of her lamp fell onto the empty bed. Made and with two neat piles of nightclothes at the end. Iris froze in the door.

"What the *hell?*"

She looked around the room again, like that would somehow reveal the mystery. Of course it did nothing of the sort. Iris turned around and stepped back into the hallway.

"Hello?!"

Nothing but a bout of rain against the window overlooking the courtyard. Where *was* everybody?

Iris tried to calm herself down just enough to *think*. This was strange. No two ways about that. Everyone gone, in the middle of the night, in this weather? Nothing normal about that. But they were *all* gone, and that meant Laura was likely with her parents. So she would be reasonably safe, wouldn't she?

Of course, that depended entirely on *where* they were, and why.

Iris raked a hand through her hair, trying to push back the beginning of a headache. First a Rose who may or may not be a secret niece, now a midnight jaunt through downright abominable weather that nobody had bothered to invite her to – or even inform her about. *None of it made sense*, and Iris wanted to scream.

Breathe. That was the key, wasn't it. Don't let this get to her. Whatever was going on, it was clearly none of her business. Despite the all but mandatory invitation, they had made this abundantly clear. And if they were so adamant that Iris knew not one tiny bit more than she absolutely had to – why should she worry about it?

Iris huffed. Of course she knew why. She couldn't *not* worry. Rather, she couldn't not *wonder*. But wondering would get her nowhere now. Asking might, if she could find the courage to.

She turned on her heel, marched back up to her room, and shut the door behind her. Oh, there were definitely things she should be asking. Perhaps she would. Tomorrow.

She put the lamp on the nightstand and went to close the curtains. At the window, she paused. At first, she thought it was lightning, and the worries were back. But no thunder sounded, even though the lights persisted. Iris squinted and peered through the sheet of rain, across the roofs and towards the edge of town. Not lightning. *Lights*. At the church.

"What the hell."

It really seemed to be that sort of night, only this time she was most definitely stone-cold sober. Someone was at the church, at this hour.

Iris worried her bottom lip. Someone was at the church. Her entire family had left the house in the middle of the night. Was she going to chalk that up to the strangest of coincidences?

Abruptly, she yanked the curtains closed and turned away from the window. Maybe she would do just that. Maybe she would ignore this, and everything else, and simply count down the days until she could get the hell out of this town and go back home.

If nobody wanted her to know anything, then why should she care to find out?

VIII

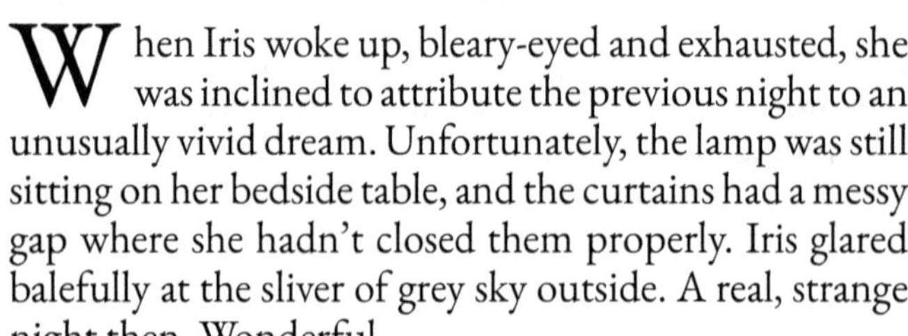

When Iris woke up, bleary-eyed and exhausted, she was inclined to attribute the previous night to an unusually vivid dream. Unfortunately, the lamp was still sitting on her bedside table, and the curtains had a messy gap where she hadn't closed them properly. Iris glared balefully at the sliver of grey sky outside. A real, strange night then. Wonderful.

Groaning, she rolled onto her back, pushed the covers aside, and went to open the window for some fresh air. It helped a little. When she was finally dressed and made her way downstairs for breakfast, she almost felt like she could think properly again.

They were already there when she entered the dining room. And worse, they all looked perfectly fine and awake and not at all like they had been out of the house in the middle of the night for who knew how long.

"Good morning, dear."

Iris puppeteered her face into a smile. "Morning."

Her father raised an eyebrow. "What, so short with us today?"

"I had a bad night." Iris made a show of hiding a yawn. "How did you sleep through all that noise?"

Her father inclined his head. "Noise?"

"The rain. It's dreadfully loud on the windows."

"Ah. Very soundly, of course." There was an odd flicker of his eyes. "You always slept through it rather well as a child."

Iris shrugged and took her seat with what was hopefully an air of indifference. "I suppose I got used to different kinds of noise."

Why the fuck are you lying to me?

Iris bit her tongue and instead acknowledged the maid unnecessarily serving her coffee with a nod. She tapped her foot until Olivia had retreated and she was finally free to fill her plate. Mostly so she had something to do, because right now, she didn't exactly have much of an appetite.

So they definitely didn't want her to know they had been gone.

"I hope the noise didn't keep you up for too long."

It was impossible to tell if the concern in her mother's voice was genuine, or as fake as Iris' tired nerves told her it was. Iris quickly shook her head.

"Not at all."

"That is good to hear." Her father cut into a breakfast sausage. "It can't be half as bad as the city noise, can it."

Iris took a bite of her eggs on toast, taking just enough time to respond to crease her father's brow. "Durham isn't so bad. It doesn't take long to get used to the streetcars."

"Streetcars." He sounded almost amused. "How worthwhile can something be if I have to pay a vehicle to take me there." He gave her a strangely pointed look. "We have never had the need for that."

"It is good exercise," her mother said, in the same tone she always had, "to walk down to the stores. It keeps you healthy, you should remember that, dear."

Iris managed a brittle laugh. "Believe me, I do plenty of walking. Who do you think stocks the shelves at the shop?"

Her father waved that off. "Nothing like a good sea breeze to keep your head clear." He cut another slice of sausage, like he was working through the food the same way he worked through conversation. "Did you enjoy your walk, by the way? Take a look around home?"

Iris tensed and put down her toast. "I'm visiting," she reminded him. "And as a visitor, I was a little underwhelmed."

"Like I said. The city is doing just fine." He sounded like he'd barely heard her. "It will be back to its old glory in no time."

"Oh, is somebody buying the hotel after all?"

Her mother's tone was sharp. The look she shared with her husband didn't escape Iris' notice. Anthony Grey cultivated a slow smile on his face.

"Why yes, I have heard that," he said. "With the hotel back up and running, we'll be having plenty more *visitors* in no time." He looked at Iris. "You really should consider visiting more often. You'd quite enjoy the break from Durham, I'm sure."

"I'm rather busy most days," Iris said cautiously. She gripped her napkin tightly. Like that would help steady her, when suddenly every word felt like a trap. "I'm not sure I can make time that easily."

"You should try during summer," her father said. "You always enjoyed the picnics, didn't you?"

"I don't think I can promise that."

Iris looked between the three of them. Her father, focused on his food. Her mother, smiling like a porcelain doll. And Laura... Sat primly, hands in her lap, and still refusing to look at her sister.

"I usually take that time to research and write."

"Naturally." Her father nodded absently. "We have an excellent library."

Something raked along the back of Iris' mind. He replied, but he didn't seem to *hear*. Neither of them did. She took a steadying breath.

"I'm not sure it can compete with the university."

"I believe Nina has curated quite the selection," her father said. "She is very discerning."

"I don't think-"

"Perhaps you could even advise her," he suggested lightly. "You certainly would have a good eye for the more specialised works."

He wasn't listening. How was he talking to her and not listening? Iris placed her palm flat on the table with a thud. "I am not coming back to Ilmoure!"

In the following silence, the sound of metal hitting wood was startlingly loud. Flinching, Iris turned to look at Laura. Her sister still wasn't looking at her. Laura carefully picked her knife off the table. There was red in her cheeks.

"Iris."

Her mother's voice snapped like a whip.

"Calm yourself. We're at the table."

Iris gaped at her. "Did you not hear a word of what I said?"

"We did."

Her father's voice was gentle. Like it had been when she was a child.

"We have heard you loud and clear." He pushed his plate aside, folding his hands on the table. "Really, in light of the recent... situation, don't you see we just want you to try again? For your sister's sake?"

Laura doesn't even give a fuck.

Iris' chair crashed to the ground as she stood abruptly. "This is me trying. If this is not enough for you, I am afraid we must all remain disappointed." She took a step back, pushing the chair further. It scratched across the floor. "Please excuse me. I need some air."

She turned on her heel and marched towards the door.

"Iris-"

Hand on the doorknob, Iris fought down a wave of nausea. "I'll see you later."

When she yanked the door open, she found the stunned face of the maid on the other side. Without a word, Iris shouldered past her and all but ran down the corridor. Someone called after her, and Iris swallowed a reply. She needed to get out. She could not spend another minute in this house.

She didn't bother closing the front door before she took the stairs down to the street. On the pavement, she halted, breath rushing too quickly through her lungs. In a moment of almost timeless suspension, she tried to calm herself, as her mother had so politely put it. Looked left and right, up and down the street. Nobody was there, but it felt like there were eyes on her, harsh and unblinking and judgemental. She needed to get *away*. Out of this forsaken town, but that road was barred to her for now. So away from the mess that was her family affairs. Just until she had herself under control again.

Abruptly, Iris turned to the left and marched up the street. To paths beyond the last row of houses. It was too early for the leisure crowds to be out and about. Maybe out there, she would find the peace she'd never feel in that cursed house.

The brisk walk up to the top of the cliffs was bordering on uncomfortable. She hadn't taken a coat or scarf to ward off the wind, so all she had was her hands in her pockets and her collar pulled up as far as it would go. Still, she made it to the top, utterly unwilling to go back and admit even the smallest defeat for something as silly as *being cold*.

What was wrong with them? Had not a single one of them paid attention in the past six years? To all the reasons why she had left this forsaken town in the first place? It sure didn't seem like it, with the way the were trying to claw her back.

If this was about the family image again, they'd find themselves starkly disappointed once more. She hadn't cared about that then, and she sure didn't care any more about it now. If they wanted to play pretend, they'd have to make do without her.

She looked out over the churning ocean. If that was even the reason. So many things they didn't tell her, things she wasn't supposed to see, and no explanation for any of it. So perhaps she needed to go and find it elsewhere. At least for her own peace of mind, she had to try.

IX

S he eventually made the walk back to town a lot slow-
er than the way up to the cliffs. Took her time to
buy a fish sandwich from the restaurant by the pier, put
together by a young man who looked much too sick to
be working. Iris refrained from commenting on it. She'd
seen him wash his hands, and that was enough for her.
With her stomach finally settling after that disaster of a
morning, she made it to the library just when she faintly
heard the lunch bell ring at the schoolhouse down the
street. At the bottom of the steps, she hesitated briefly.
It was no use. If she wanted answers, she'd best get to
looking for them.

She found Cateleya behind the front desk, where she
was taking notes in a heavy-looking ledger. A skinny,
sand-coloured cat was stretched out before her, allowing
her to occasionally run a hand through its fur while it
purred up a storm.

At Iris' approach, Cateleya looked up.

"Iris." She put down her pen. "What are you doing
here?"

Desperate to stall the inevitable, Iris nodded at the
cat, whose yellow eyes were half open and peering at her

in that half-hearted way that exuded both curiosity and dignified indifference. "Is that the library mascot?"

Cateleya huffed out a laugh. "You could call him that. He lives somewhere in the area and keeps wandering in when the doors are open. Nina complains, but she's also too cheap to buy more rat traps, so he's practically working here." She scratched the cat behind his ear, and he somehow grew a little longer still, toes spread and head squished into Cateleya's hand. "The kids love him, so he'll stay no matter what. They named him Breadstick."

"Breadstick." Iris eyed the cat, trying not to laugh despite herself. "I can see that."

Cateleya folded her hands in front of her. Again – impossible to ignore. Still – too afraid to ask. "So, what are you doing here?"

It sounded a lot more curious than hostile, which was the only reason Iris didn't run right then and there. Instead, she took a deep breath and tried to stay calm – for now.

"I was hoping you'd have a minute." She glanced around, but the foyer was empty aside from the both of them. "It's about Rose."

"Shouldn't you be asking your sister?"

Iris bit back a hysterical little giggle. "I should be, shouldn't I." She crossed her arms, tapping an impatient rhythm against the diamond floor. "They won't talk to me. It's... weird. I don't think I should be asking."

Cateleya sighed. "Iris, I'm at work, I don't have time for games."

"It's not a game!" Iris tugged at the roots of her hair to fend off another headache. "I looked for her. For Rose. In the pictures, and in the graveyard. She's not there."

"What do you mean, she's not there?" Cateleya folded her hands on the ledger. "Did they take down her pictures?"

"I don't know. Maybe?" Iris shook her head. "That's not the weird part. There is no grave. I looked. And I know where Matthew is buried, I was there, but there is no Rose Alden buried in the entire graveyard. I even asked the preacher, he said he didn't know anyone by that name."

"That's... odd." Cateleya's eyes flickered around the room. "He's not usually forgetful about his flock."

"Wouldn't know that, would I," Iris muttered. "I know how this sounds, but I feel like I'm going crazy." She loathed how much it sounded like a plea, but that was why she was here. "You weren't messing with me, were you?"

Cateleya raised her chin. "Why in the world would I joke about something like that?"

"I don't know!" Iris raked a hand through her hair. "But she's not buried with Matthew. Nobody has ever told me about her. There's no grave."

"You must have missed it." Cateleya shook her head. "I met her."

Iris tried to ignore how much that hurt.

"Rose is real, Iris, I don't know what else to tell you." Cateleya's tone became gentle. "Maybe Laura doesn't like to talk about her."

"But she talks about-" Iris shut her mouth with a click. Had she? Had Laura said a single word about her own son in Iris' presence? "She had no problem with me talking about Matthew."

"But she wasn't the one to invite you to his funeral."

Iris paused. "No." She bit her lip. "You honestly think she'd do that? Pretend Rose never existed?"

"I know another Grey sister who is very good indeed at avoiding difficult discussions," Cateleya said pointedly. "I thought you would've asked by now."

"Ah." Iris cleared her throat, her gaze dipping down ever so briefly. "I figured you might not want me to mention it."

"You wouldn't be entirely wrong," Cateleya admitted. "We haven't exactly *told* anyone yet."

Iris hesitated for a moment. "We? Who's the lucky someone?"

Cateleya shrugged. "You wouldn't know him. He moved here after you left."

It sounded so dismissive, Iris didn't dare ask again.

Cateleya, now serious again, pushed away from the desk and motioned for Iris to join her. "Follow me."

So Iris did, into one of the empty side rooms where Cateleya turned left right behind the door.

"Children's section," Cateleya said. "It's where we hang the pictures from the summer festivals." She walked along the frames hung on the wall until she reached the end of the row. "Here. That was two years ago. Matthew won a raffle. She should be... there."

Iris squinted at the black-and-white picture, where Cateleya was pointing. It was a small group of children lined up in front of their parents, proudly displaying the books they would be taking home. Matthew was standing to the left, with a wide grin and wind-swept hair. Behind him, Laura was looking much more reserved. On her hip, she was holding a child no older than two. Without colour, there wasn't much detail to make out, but the little girl had the same dark hair and pale eyes as her mother. The same as her aunt, whom she'd never met.

"I don't understand. Is that really her daughter?"

"It is. I promise you that's the truth."

She'd known Cateleya as a lot of things, but never as a liar. The brief shame Iris felt, now that she knew, that she had even considered the possibility of this being a prank, made way for something else, something she couldn't quite pin down just yet.

"Why would they hide her like this?" Iris finally looked away from the picture. "I understand that they didn't tell me while I was away, I do, but there's nothing. Nobody mentioned her, there are no pictures in the house... Why would they do that?"

Cateleya breathed a weary sigh. "You might want to ask them, not me."

Iris flinched at the idea, but nodded. "Of course. I should. I will. I just needed to..."

She fell silent when a staccato of footfalls approached from the foyer.

"Cat?"

Cateleya's expression shifted strangely for a moment. Iris tried to ignore how the privilege of her old nickname had now moved to somebody else.

"In here!" Cateleya called out. A moment later, the teacher Mr. Mason poked his head through the door.

"Oh!" He looked rather sheepishly between them. "My apologies, I didn't know you were busy."

"We're-"

"I'm not-"

They both fell silent, and Cateleya arched an eyebrow at Iris, who ducked her head and motioned a silent 'go on'.

"I'm not busy. What is it?"

He fully stepped into the room. "Well, I was *intending* to ask if you would like to go out for lunch, but if there is something you are doing right now, then I won't intrude." He gave Iris a curt little nod. "Miss Grey."

Cateleya's eyes narrowed in that way Iris remembered all too well. "You've met?"

"We have," Iris replied. "Mr. Mason, ah, made an appearance at Matthew's wake."

He had the good grace to look embarrassed. "Yes, I did, didn't I." He cleared his throat. "I do apologise for the way I went about it. I shouldn't have asked questions this publicly."

Iris crossed her arms. "Probably not, no." She studied him, uneasy at the memory but with a strange sense of urgency digging at the back of her mind. "Why did you, though? I don't suppose you were just trying to ruin the event and upset my sister."

Now he seemed taken aback. "I was not!"

Cateleya blew out a sharp breath. "Don't tell me you went and asked about what happened to Matthew *at his wake?*"

Iris looked from one to the other. "I take it this is not the first... incident?"

"There are no *incidents*," Mr. Mason said primly. "Something is happening to Ilmoure's children. Richard asked me to come and teach for a reason, and I can't just sit back and watch this happen to my students!"

"Watch what happen?" An uneasy knot settled into Iris' stomach, a feeling that was quickly becoming much too familiar. "Are you saying something *happened* to Matthew?"

"Nothing happened to Matthew," Cateleya cut it. She pinched the bridge of her nose. "I'm sorry, I don't have time for lunch today, I have paperwork to catch up on." She looked sternly between the two of them. "Now, unless either of you need a book, I need to get back to work."

Her tone kept Iris' mouth shut rather thoroughly. It seemed that she was not the only one. Mr. Mason ducked his head and raised his hands.

"Apologies, dear. I'll be going."

And go he did, right back out where he had come from. Iris stared after him for a moment, torn between what he had implied about her nephew – and the way he had called Cateleya 'dear'.

"Iris." Cateleya fixed her with a rather steely look. "I meant that."

"Right. Sorry." Iris took a shaky breath. "Thank you. For showing me the picture."

And with that, she turned and hurried out of the room, crossed the foyer and took the stairs two steps at a time. In front of the now-empty schoolhouse, she caught up with her prey.

"Mr. Mason!"

He stopped and turned, his surprise obvious. "Can I help you, Miss Grey?"

"You just might." Iris came to a stop a few feet away. "I'd like to take that lunch with you instead. My treat." She glanced over her shoulder, up and down the empty street. "I'd really like to talk to you."

It was profoundly uncomfortable, the silence as they walked to the pier, sat down in the restaurant, and made their orders under the baleful gaze of the sickly young man cleaning the counter. Iris waited until the gloomy-looking waitress had served them their drinks and disappeared back into the kitchen, and the pale man had followed. Only then did she attempt a conversation.

"I suppose you want to know why I dragged you here."

He chuckled. "Dragged is such a strong word, isn't it." He leaned on the table. "I assume this is about what I said at the library."

"For the most part." Iris slowly turned the glass in front of her, wondering if those little smears were on the inside or on the outside of it. "You said something is wrong with the children here. That's why you were at the wake."

"Ah." A touch of red crept into his cheeks. "I really am sorry for the way that went. And, uhm. About the other time. I didn't mean to spook you in the woods."

Iris exhaled sharply. "If I'm being perfectly honest, I don't care about any of that."

"You... do not."

Very briefly, Iris wondered if she should go into detail. Explain why, exactly she could not bring herself to care right this minute about whether or not her sister or her parents might have been upset by the intrusion. In the end, she decided on a rather sullen: "Family history."

He ducked his head. "I see."

Iris wasn't sure he really did, but it seemed to be a satisfactory explanation to him, and that was all that mattered. She leaned in a little so she could keep her voice down in the empty restaurant.

"I want to know what's going on with this place." She thought of the photograph, the smiling boy and his little sister. "I know Matthew was sick. Nobody told me what it was. You know something about that?"

"I know as much as the next person," he said cautiously. "Although I'm trying to find out more." An edge of frustration crept into his voice. "People seem rather uninterested in that. Some might even say that I'm meddling in things I shouldn't be meddling in."

"Are you?"

"These are my students," he said curtly. "When they keep disappearing, I'm going to ask questions!"

"Disappearing?" Iris was taken aback. "I thought they were getting sick."

His smile was razor-thin. "They are. You see, there is this illness that seems to be going around. It's very localised, and affects children the most. So I see it happen in my classroom. Sometimes..." He looked at her oddly. "Sometimes, they are like your nephew. Others, they start showing signs, and their parents pull them out of school. So I ask. Do they need assistance, materials, course work? And I am told not to worry. That they don't need anything. And that is usually the last I ever hear about it."

"They don't come back when they get better?"

"No." He paused. "I have no evidence that they ever do get better."

Iris swallowed thickly. "So they die. Like Matthew."

"That is just it. They don't seem to." He tapped the scratched tabletop. "There are no funerals. Not as many as there should be, anyway." He grew a little pale under his blush. "I know how this sounds. But I watch the graveyard. These children just disappear entirely. They don't come back, they don't die. I don't know what happens to them."

Oh, this did not sound pleasant at all. "Are they being sent to a sanatorium, perhaps?" Maybe that was it. Maybe that was where Rose was. "If they are so sick-"

"I thought so, too. But why not tell me that?" He shook his head. "I have asked old university friends of mine, in the medical field. They don't know a thing about this. Nobody has ever even heard about an illness that only affects a single town. They think it's nonsense, and I must be missing some kind of obvious explanation."

Iris wished rather fiercely for a moment that this was in fact the truth. "But you don't think that you are."

He nodded bleakly. "There has to be-"

He abruptly fell silent when the door to the kitchen bumped into the wall and the waitress stalked over with their food. She set both plates down with just a little bit more force than necessary and left them again without saying a single word.

"Well, there goes my drink order."

They busied themselves with their meal while the waitress moved around behind the bar, clinking glasses and wiping down the surfaces almost aggressively. Iris was halfway through her portion when the woman finally decided to return to the kitchen and left them alone in blessed silence.

"What do you think is happening to those kids?" Iris glanced up, catching his eye for a moment. "The ones that leave but don't die."

"I wish I knew. I haven't been able to find out, or find a trace of even a single one of them." He hesitated for a moment, then put down his cutlery. "Why are you so interested in this? Your nephew...."

He fell silent, and Iris shook her head. "He... is dead, I know that much." She bit her lip. "He wasn't my sister's only child. Cateleya said she had a daughter. Younger than Matthew, so she wouldn't have been in school yet. She..." Iris blew out a breath. "According to Cateleya, the girl died. According to Father Melville, there is no Rose Alden buried in Ilmoure."

He seemed startled. "You think Cat invented her?"

"I don't think she did, that is the whole problem," Iris muttered. "That's why I'm here. I feel like I'm going crazy, but if there is something going on, then maybe whatever it is got Rose, too."

And if this was indeed the case, and this was not a load of unfounded nonsense as Mr. Mason's colleagues had so helpfully suggested...

Did Laura know about it all? Was she a part of what-ever was happening to the town's children?

"I wish I had more to tell you," he said, "but for now, this is all I have. I'm just glad someone does not imme-diately inform me that I probably had a glass too many last night."

It was a lot more than Iris had in the morning, and it already felt like too much. Too much to add to the tension in the house, to her father's questions and her mother's fake smiles and Laura's silence. To whatever they had been up to in the middle of the night that Iris had not been allowed to be a part of.

It all seemed too much. And yet, Iris couldn't help but wonder if she hadn't just started to see the full picture.

Despite Mr. Mason's insistence to the contrary, Iris kept her promise and paid for their meal. There hadn't been much else to say. At least it was easy enough to be quiet around him. When they'd left the restaurant into an overcast early afternoon, they exchanged a polite good-bye before he turned to head back to the schoolhouse.

Only then Iris finally found the courage to bring it up. "Mr. Mason."

He stopped and turned back to her, a smile curled around his mouth. "Henry, please."

She nodded in acknowledgment. "Henry. I was just..." She took a deep breath. "Cateleya. Who is she to you?"

"Ah." He seemed a little sheepish. "I do know the history, so please believe me that I am not trying to get a rise out of you."

The phrasing had Iris on edge in an instant. "Mean-ing?"

"We have been involved since shortly after I moved here."

"...oh."

Involved. He said it so casually, like she should have expected it. And maybe she should have. She had no right to feel this crushed about it, had she.

"I wasn't aware."

"We chose not to make anything official." He sighed deeply. "It rather seems like Cateleya is more opposed than ever lately."

"I see." Iris managed to plaster a smile onto her face. "I was just... wondering, is all." She bobbed her head. "Sorry. Didn't mean to hold you up. I'll be seeing you."

And with that, she all but fled the scene, with yet another thing wedged into her mind that felt like it would stay there for a while. Well, that was what she got for asking. Should've held her tongue. It wasn't her business anymore, after all.

And was it even important? If this man, and her own eyes, were to be believed, something was going on in this town that nobody seemed to care about at all. Something that took people's children, and it barely seemed to bother them. It wasn't even talked about. How was that possible? Shouldn't this be making news? Headlines all the way to Durham, if a new illness was spreading from Ilmoure as its source? And yet – nothing.

And none of this even took into account all of those children that allegedly vanished into thin air one day, never to come back.

Hands in her pockets, Iris wandered down the promenade just so she didn't have to be still. It was madness, laid out like that. The kind of theory cooked up by unwashed people balancing on soap boxes and yelling about the end of the world. Only this was an educated man, someone who Cateleya trusted enough to be *in-*

volved with, someone who had sounded so utterly convinced and concerned by it all that it was difficult to dismiss it. And she couldn't pretend that she hadn't seen the empty beds and the lights from the church herself. The lack of evidence that a child, her niece, had ever existed beyond that single picture at the library.

Certainly *something* was happening in this forsaken town. She just had to figure out where to start looking.

X

She was loath to return home, but return, she had to, so Iris slunk back to the house in the late afternoon. Olivia's greeting was perfectly polite – and nothing more. Her mother's pointed look as Iris entered the family room was much, much worse.

"Have you calmed yourself?"

"Hello, mother." It was all Iris could do not to sound openly sarcastic. "I'm feeling much better, thank you for asking."

"Good." Katherine nodded curtly. "Now, go and make yourself presentable, dinner will be served early today. We're having a guest."

For a moment, Iris forgot to be sullen. "A guest?"

"Father Melville is joining us. I expect everyone to be on their best behaviour."

Impossible to say if that was directed at her, or if her mother simply didn't trust anyone to behave themselves. So Iris kept her reaction to a nod, mumbled an excuse that earned her another admonishing look, and retreated upstairs to 'wash up' – and prepare herself for that dinner.

Despite everything in her begging to simply crawl into bed and wait for Friday, Iris joined her family in the dining room with little appetite and a smile; the kind she put on when she was roughly two minutes away from jeopardising her job in the face of one too many belligerent customers.

It seemed to be sufficient. When she entered the dining room, her father was just taking his seat, turning halfway to the door in the process.

"Iris!" He gestured at the empty chair at the end of the table. "Please, take your seat, the soup is about to be served."

"Apologies." Iris did as she had been asked. "I wasn't aware we'd be eating early today."

The preacher, sitting to her father's left, smiled thinly. "That would be my fault, I believe. I made an unannounced visit and your mother generously invited me to stay."

"Always a good host, my Katherine," her father said. "Iris, you remember Father Robert Melville?"

"I do," Iris replied quietly. And from the way he studied her, so did he. "We have met."

"Excellent!" Anthony gestured across the table. "Father, this is my wayward oldest, Iris." He looked at her jovially. "She has left our beautiful Ilmoure to go and study in the great, big city of Durham. Has built a proper life for herself, or so I have heard. Even has her name in magazines, if you can believe it!"

"Is that so." Father Melville inclined his head. "A pleasure to meet you properly, Miss Grey."

"Likewise, Father."

Olivia chose this exact moment to appear with the soup, which gave Iris a few minutes to acclimate while the soup was being served, tasted, and judged excellent. Her mother seemed rather concerned with everything being to Father Melville's tastes, which he kept assuring her it was.

"I have never been served a single crumb of sub-par food in your house, dear Katherine." He took a piece of bread and tore it in half, careful to hold it over his soup plate as he did. "Your family have never been anything but perfect hosts."

"Naturally," her father agreed. "We're honoured to have you around, Father." He chuckled. "We would not dare be anything else."

"And this dedication humbles me." Father Melville smiled his narrow smile again. "I would be quite pleased to see more of it in the future. Will I be seeing you again as well, Miss Grey?"

Iris nearly dropped her spoon into the soup. Years of manners lessons under her mother kept her hand just steady enough to avoid embarrassment. "Pardon?"

"Your lovely sister is married, and will soon be quite busy again," the preacher said, "and your dear father would surely like to retire in due time. I was under the impression that it might fall to you to take over managing the family estate."

Iris' fingers tightened around the spoon. This was certainly the first time she heard about that. "I'm afraid that is not the case, Father."

"We have not talked about that just yet," her father quickly said. "For now, Iris is scheduled to return to Durham on Friday."

"Is that so."

The way he said it sent a shiver down Iris' spine. She felt scrutinised, ready to go on the defensive for not a single obvious reason. She loathed the feeling. "My job won't wait, I'm afraid." She put down her spoon and folded her hands in her lap. "I can't stay on such short notice."

Nor did she plan to stay at all. They exchanged a look, her father and this preacher who was sitting next to him as if this was *his* house. Once again, Iris found herself longing for Friday, and for that uncomfortable seat on a bus nobody wanted her on. At least this time, once she got off she could simply never get back on.

"Such a shame," Father Melville finally said. "I do believe that family should remain close. Our community so benefits from a sense of unity."

Her father's laughter sounded strangely uncomfortable to her ears. "A shame indeed, but we must let our children go, mustn't we. They will find their way eventually."

"It certainly seems so." Father Melville looked up sharply. "So, Miss Grey, now I must confess that I am curious. Where is it that your way has led you in Durham?"

Iris felt a little dizzy trying to keep up. "The university."

"Naturally." The way his expression changed from guarded guest to indulgent family friend set Iris on edge. "I myself attended when I was young, if you can believe that."

"Hm."

Iris began eating again on the off chance that he might take it as the hint she meant it as. He, unfortunately, did not.

"Although I am glad that my own path has led me to such an appreciative flock." He levelled an inquisitive look at her. "It is difficult to find this kind of unified community in a place like Durham, is it not?"

"I wouldn't know." Iris looked down at her food. "I don't attend service that much anymore."

"Ah." His tone almost made her look up again. Not surprised – disappointed. She didn't even know the man. "A shame, really."

Through the soup and the main course, Iris managed to hold what passed for a conversation. Every sentence, almost every word, she caught and weighed before she replied, searching for something that she couldn't pinpoint. There was no reason for any of it to bother her this much. Yet when they finally reached the last dregs of coffee after a too-sweet dessert, she was about ready to bolt. To her endless relief, Father Melville appeared equally ready to call it a night.

"I do need to be going." He stood, as did her father. "Thank you ever so much for your hospitality, Anthony." He nodded at her mother. "Katherine."

For Laura and Iris herself, he had another one of those little smiles, a nod, and then her father escorted him outside. Not a moment later, Laura and her mother got up as if their chairs had caught fire.

"Excuse me." Katherine was already by the door. "There is something that needs my attention."

And gone she was. Laura followed, lingering only a moment with a strangely empty look at Iris. "I'm rather tired tonight." She swallowed thickly. "I'll be retiring now."

With that, she all but fled the room. Iris was left alone, head spinning and once again feeling like she was walking on thin ice, never knowing when it would crack under her feet.

Nothing made sense anymore in this place.

"Good night to you, too," Iris muttered as she finally left the table herself. She should be glad, she reasoned. All the more time for her to hide in her room and try to make time pass faster.

She went through the motions, changed and brushed hair and teeth and eventually all but tiptoed her way back to her room. Perhaps it was that which allowed her to catch her mother by surprise at the foot of the stairs.

"Iris." Katherine paused, an odd look in her eyes. "Are you retiring early?"

"It's been a long day."

Her mother's mouth twitched. "It has been." She nodded curtly. "Good night, dear."

Katherine had already turned away, and Iris wasn't sure what possessed her. Maybe it was the desperation of not knowing where her sanity began and ended anymore when it came to her own family. "Mother."

Katherine froze, and for a second, Iris wondered if she would bolt. Eventually, she looked back at Iris. "Yes?"

"I was just wondering." Iris felt her throat tighten uncomfortably. It took her a moment to figure out what to say. "I've been to the library. There's an exhibition, and I saw a photograph. When Matthew won a raffle at a festival?"

Katherine became motionless in front of her. "Iris, isn't it a bit late to-"

"Laura was in it, you know?" Iris quickly continued, keeping her eyes locked with her mother's as if that would keep Katherine from fleeing – and make her give her an honest answer. "She was holding a little girl." She paused ever so briefly, but nothing moved in Katherine's face. "Is she Audrey's? I didn't know she was married. I'd like to congratulate, if it's not-"

"Audrey doesn't have children." Katherine took a deep breath and raised her chin. "She doesn't even live here anymore."

The dread that clawed into Iris' stomach was a sudden and visceral feeling that she hadn't expected in its intensity. Not an answer, really – but an answer nonetheless. "Are you certain? She looked so much like-"

"Your cousin moved away years ago." A dangerous glint entered Katherine's eyes. "You must be mistaken."

The words died on Iris' tongue. *How could I be mistaken when she looks just like us?* She kept that to herself. Regretted even asking. Too late now.

"I'm sorry." Although what for, she wasn't quite sure. "Must've been the black and white."

Katherine nodded stiffly. "You should be more careful next time. You could have upset your sister if you had asked her instead."

Iris bit her lip. Matthew. Again, she was unable to recall if Laura had spoken a single word about her own son the whole time Iris had been here. "Of course. I'll be more careful."

"I'm sure she will appreciate it." Abruptly, Katherine took a step back. "I will see you at breakfast."

It sounded like one last command before she turned away and walked down the hall, a clear dismissal. Iris ducked her head and hurried back upstairs, shutting the door to her room with aching relief.

Not an answer, and yet it seemed like confirmation to her. It wasn't, she kept telling herself as she went about closing the curtains. She couldn't rely on a gut feeling and the words of an ex who might be holding a grudge. And yet. What reason would Cateleya have to lie?

It was most definitely a miracle that she managed to fall asleep rather quickly. All the more upsetting then that she woke abruptly, from what, she wasn't quite sure. Groggily, Iris turned on her back, trying to get her head above what felt like murky water. She yawned heartily, blinking into the pitch black. Fantastic. Just what she needed.

She wasn't sure how long she lay there, waiting for sleep to come back. Instead, she felt more awake by the minute. Eventually, her frustration got the better of her. Iris threw the covers aside with enough force to toss them off the bed entirely, failed to find her slippers in the dark, and left her room to get either a glass of water or brandy. She'd decide once she got to the kitchen.

She never even got that far. When she came down the stairs, skipping the creaky ones this time, she found the hallway illuminated from below – the lights in the entrance hall were on, and somebody was talking. Iris halted at the top of the stairs. Tried to assure herself that it was unlikely to be an intruder. They'd be quieter, and not bother with the lights.

Whoever it was, Iris was not keen on chit-chatting in the middle of the night. Teetering on the top step, she tried to decide whether to go back to her room with empty hands. Tempting, but so was the brandy.

"...convince Iris?"

Her own name froze her where she was. So it was her mother. She couldn't help but strain to listen.

"We can't." Her father's brusque tone was surprising. "She's not like that. She needs time. Make the choice herself."

Her mother scoffed. "She never will, Anthony, you know that. She has no interest in men, let alone in settling back home."

"Do you think I forgot?" her father replied sharply. "What is your alternative? Force?"

"If we have to."

A chill ran down Iris spine. Force? Force her to do what? Come home to manage that damn estate?

Iris took a breath as deep as she dared. They couldn't. They had nothing to hold over her anymore.

Her father exhaled sharply. "She might not even *be* the same as Laura."

"We can't risk that," her mother snapped. "Think about it. Laura and Audrey. Four ascended between the two of them. Only one who didn't, and it wasn't Laura's." There was steel in her mother's voice again. "If it really runs in the family, we need to make sure she does her part. Father Melville agrees."

"So do I!"

There was movement towards the stairs, and Iris flinched back into the shadows of the hallway. Mind racing, but just aware enough to know that she couldn't be found now.

"We'll bring her around. It's easier if she makes the choice herself. We have some time."

"We might not. She's asking questions."

"Questions?"

"About Rose."

A poignant pause. "How did she find out?"

"We forgot a picture. In the library."

Another sigh. Weary, now. "I see. We'll handle it. But not tonight. We have a ceremony to attend."

More movement, a click of the lock. Then: "Laura?"

There was an odd moment of quiet before Laura's soft voice just barely made it up to where Iris was standing.

"I'm coming."

A draft of chill air wafted up the stairs, catching Iris by surprise. She clamped a hand on her mouth to keep a startled little gasp at bay. Again when the lights went out, plunging the house into darkness once more. She remained where she was, motionless, heart beating a staccato in her chest, until she heard the front door close. With a strangled whimper, she leaned heavily against the wall, dizzy and nauseous and unsure why she was either.

What in the world had that been about? The estate? Why? Why were they so bent on having her come *home*, come back to this town that never wanted her in the first place?

Iris closed her eyes as the back of her head hit the wall with a dull thud. It wasn't all. Couldn't be all. But noth-

ing else made sense. *Ascended*. Like Laura and Audrey –
who didn't even live here anymore. Why bring her up?
What did Iris have to do with any of it?

What did it have to do with her non-existent interest
in men?

A faint whisper of an idea brushed against her mind,
and Iris resolutely shut it down. Refused to consider it a
possibility. They knew, had known for a long time, that
they were not getting that from her. They had Laura,
which had to be enough. And it had been – until now?
A cold knot formed in Iris' stomach. No. That could *not*
be it. Even Katherine Grey would not go this far.

And all that said – where in the world had they gone
at this hour, anyway?

Without answers, without even so much as a direction
to look in to find some, Iris pushed herself away from
the wall. Fumbled in the dark until she made it back upstairs, bumped her knee into her door frame, and finally
slammed the door closed behind her, leaving her in the
darkness of her room.

She leaned against the wood while her eyes adjusted to
the faint light coming from the window. She stumbled
over, all but tearing the curtains aside to get some fresh
air and clear her head.

Hand on the window latch, Iris gaped at the lights
outside.

The church. Again. If she'd been gracious enough
to attribute it to an absurd coincidence the last time,
tonight, she did not feel as charitable. There was too
much strange behaviour to consider, too many mysteries
to unravel, too much secrecy to ignore. Tonight, Iris
could not help but wonder – why were they going to
church at this hour?

Iris pushed herself away from the door. Perhaps she
was not getting most of the answers she was so desper-

ately looking for. But she could get at least one, right now, if she hurried.

XI

The chill of the night clung to her uncomfortably, almost like a fog but not quite yet. Maybe a foggy night would have made this easier. Less nerve-wracking while Iris darted from corner to corner, looking left and right and over her shoulder for any sign that she'd been seen. That the streets were not as deserted as they looked. Nothing stirred as she made her way towards the church.

They were not there, she kept telling herself. They were out for a walk, she tried to convince her wired nerves. They had never left the house, and she had been seeing things the entire time, she thought, just once. She knew what she'd seen, tonight and since she'd gotten off that bus. She might not know what to make of it, but it was real, and she had to get to the bottom of it. If for no other reason than she was apparently to be involved, regardless of her own wishes in the matter. That, she could not ignore.

When she reached Church Road, she slowed to as silent a walk as she could muster. For a split second before she turned the corner, she once again briefly wondered if she indeed had seen what she'd seen. If she wouldn't find the church dark and quiet and herself looking the fool. She almost laughed in hysterical relief when she saw the lights twinkling from the looming silhouette of the church. Hand on her mouth, she stood by the corner for what felt like an eternity until she could convince herself to move again. Now that she was here, now that she knew her mind wasn't cracking, she had to know. Had to see, so she would know what to do next. Maybe.

She took care to walk next to the gravel on the damp grass. In the silence all around, she did not dare make a sound. To her overly anxious mind, it felt like a single misstep might well be her doom.

It was fine. Just one look. Just to see if her hunch was correct. She'd take one look, and then she'd leave and never look back.

She approached the church in a wide loop from the side. With the way the light cast out from the stained-glass windows, it was impossible to tell if the shadows she saw were monuments or guards. They did not move, in any case, as Iris closed in on the one clear glass window of the building. Her one chance to get a good look inside.

She pressed herself into the dark wedges between two windows. Standing still, even over the rush of blood in her ears she heard the noises from within. Droning murmurs interspersed with a single, solitary voice. The preacher, although he spoke in a way that made him barely recognisable. Iris didn't understand a single word he was saying.

Throat dry and chest fluttering, she turned around and steadied her hands on the decorative outcropping in front of her. Just wide enough to tiptoe on, and just high enough to peer inside, if she could get up.

It took three attempts, and after each failure, Iris froze momentarily, listening, expecting to be discovered. Nothing moved around her. So she tried again. When she finally found purchase, she steadied herself, rose, and looked through the window.

She wasn't sure what she had expected. A packed church, a throng of people, crowds like on the pier, once upon a time. Instead, she found the church half empty, with people spread out among the pews. Some, too many, that she knew. Mr. and Mrs. Dixon from a few houses down. Dennis Caldwell, who had been her father's business partner since she was a child. His son right next to him. The mayor, of all people. Mr. Belafonte and his wife Eleanor, who had raised Cateleya as her own. It gave Iris a start seeing them here, involved in... whatever it might be they were doing. But they were not who she was looking for. Almost frantic in her search, Iris kept looking, row after row, until she stopped, biting down on her lip. They were all here. Laura with her head bent, hands on her belly. Her parents looking straight ahead, at Father Melville.

The preacher was standing behind the altar, which seemed the only thing left that Iris recognised. The old wooden artwork had been removed, as had the embroidered cloth. Something small and shiny sat on the bare altar. A chalice, Iris realised after a moment.

Father Melville wore a robe of dark blue that had nothing in common with what he had worn at the funeral. He was holding a book in one hand that was certainly not a bible, and in the other – a knife. Above him, a symbol fashioned from gold so large and looming it dominated the space. The only thing it had in common with a cross was its prominent place in the building.

The symbol she'd seen in the salon in her parents' house, what now felt like a lifetime ago.

Iris couldn't make out what Father Melville was saying – even if she'd understood, the blood rushing in her ears would've drowned it out. She felt woozy, but kept clinging to the outcropping as she watched. Odd gestures, interspersed with loud, clear exclamations answered by the attendees. Worshippers. Whatever this was.

When movement rippled through them, Iris ducked away briefly, a gasp stuck in her throat until she realised they were walking, one by one, towards the altar. And one by one, they picked up the chalice and drank what was inside. As they did so, Father Melville held out the knife to them. After each one had put down the chalice, they wrapped their fingers around the knife. Soon enough, it became apparent that they were all drawing blood. Even the handful of sickly-looking children in the crowd, too young to be up at this hour. Too young to protest being here. They moved like puppets under their parents' watchful eyes.

If this was communion, it certainly wasn't anything Iris had ever seen before.

When a woman Laura's age and just as pregnant walked up to the altar, the process became different. Father Melville smiled at her. Took her hands in his. His lips moved, but now, Iris couldn't hear a thing. The woman bent her head. Then, she drank from the chalice, held the knife, and returned to her seat. After three more people, Laura walked up, and Father Melville did the same.

When Laura's fingers closed around the blade, Iris turned away and dropped back to the ground. All she wanted was to hurl into a nearby bush, but instead, she staggered away, back to where she'd come from, reeling and nauseous and trying to make sense of it all.

This was not the church she'd gone to as a child. There was no telling when it had changed – or into what. What it was now could not be in any way considered to be normal. Had they forgotten about the part where the blood was purely symbolic these days?

She suppressed a near-hysterical laugh. Of course they hadn't. None of this had looked accidental. They were doing this with a purpose, though what that could be, Iris couldn't begin to fathom. All she knew that her own family were wrapped up in it, and if she was not gravely mistaken, they were intending to pull her into it, too.

Whether she wanted to or not.

She stopped by the first corner that afforded her a measure of obfuscation and looked back. At the church that was a church no more. And as she did, the lights inside changed. Iris shrunk back into the shadows but found herself unable to tear her eyes away, to turn and move and *run*. The doors opened, and the congregation exited, led by Father Melville and followed by the rest in a peculiar order. Behind Father Melville walked Laura and the other pregnant woman, smiling so serenely. After them came the children – and the young man from the diner. He looked so sick in the strange light, but held his head high and proud as he walked in the procession. Behind him came the rest of this most bizarre parish. Some bent their heads, then walked away, heading for one of the churchyard gates. The rest stayed together, moving towards the gate nearest Iris. They were carrying lanterns and moving in silence along the paths, the only sound their steps on the gravel. When they reached the gate, Iris' heart skipped a beat before she realised they were not heading in her direction. Instead, as if everything else that Iris had witnessed tonight wasn't unsettling enough already, they turned away from the churchyard and moved along the street towards the edge of town.

Against all better judgment, with a knot in her stomach and her neck prickling cold, Iris watched until they had disappeared behind a corner. Then, she followed.

She kept her distance, always out of sight. In the dead of night with the streets deserted, it was almost easier to follow the trailing light than the people themselves, so Iris did just that. Beyond the last row of houses, up the path along the cliff and into the woods. It got more difficult here, and she had to gain more distance to avoid being discovered. Her blood ran cold at what might happen if she was, but at the same time, an almost feverish compulsion kept her going. They passed by the benches, the sea beyond a calm obsidian plane stretching to the horizon. Further up, and up, and finally – the sharp bend up to the old mine.

Iris gaped up the path when she realised that this was where they'd gone. Nevertheless, she kept following. Lights and murmurs up ahead, growing louder as she approached, ducking from bush to tree to bush again. When she got close enough to glimpse them, she stopped. At the same time, something else was added to the noise. A grinding sound, the rattling of metal – and guttural noises that could not possibly be coming from a human throat.

It was difficult to discern who was who from Iris' less than advantageous hiding spot. Eventually, the group shifted, moving away from the entrance to the mine to allow a second group to emerge. When the light from the lanterns caught their features, Iris had to force herself into silence.

Whatever it was, it had to be what had made those sounds, because this was human in only the vaguest sense. It walked on two legs, had two arms and a head with a face. It also had glossy, steel-grey skin, long fingers tipped with razor nails, and a tuft of what appeared to be feathers on its head, gleaming a reddish bronze from the light. It left the mines with more like it in tow, large, dark eyes wandering over the gathered congregation. Iris resisted the urge to duck away when those eyes strayed briefly over the trees. Movement would betray her for sure. Rooted in place, she might just survive.

Those black pits returned to the human crowd, and to Father Melville at last. More of those odd sounds were produced, and Father Melville replied in kind. He stepped sideways and made a sweeping gesture – at Laura.

Iris pressed a hand to her mouth to stifle a scream. Heart hammering, she couldn't turn her eyes away. Laura did not look afraid. She was smiling again, like she had in the church, and last before that during the wake. This time, there was tension there, just enough to be noticeable. The creature held her gaze, then nodded. Stepped aside, and two more came forward, much smaller and moving awkwardly, like they were only just coming into their unnaturally long limbs. Despite their same freakish appearance, the differences were impossible to ignore. Bright silver eyes, and instead of copper on their heads, it was an inky black gently swaying back and forth with their uneven movement. They tottered forward, past the tall one, past Father Melville – right into Laura's open arms.

Iris felt dizzy as she watched the scene unfold. Watched as Laura's smile brightened, as she embraced those monstrous things like-

Children.

The horrifying idea clawed its way into Iris' mind and took unbidden root.

Not silver – grey eyes. Not feathers – black hair. Like Laura. Like Audrey. Like herself.

She bit her hand, tasting copper. Laura held them like children – because they were. The children she'd lost. The one Iris had watched buried, and the one she was never meant to know about.

No.

Impossible.

Laura pressed a kiss to the smaller one's head, and it rested its hand on her cheek. It looked past her, then, at someone else in the crowd. Anthony Grey moved to kneel next to his daughter and-

Grandchildren.

-to wrap his arms around them all. Murmurs arose from the crowd, and more creatures dispersed, to greetings and moments like the one that had put ice-cold dread into Iris' heart. A cacophony of grunts and low voices filled the air, until Father Melville's voice cut through it.

"Let's go inside. We have rain coming."

The group moved almost as one. Clustered around the entrance, tall silhouettes towering until, one after the other, they ducked through the gate and inside, where the darkness soon swallowed the last remnants of light. Left outside in the dark, Iris leaned against a tree and closed her eyes.

No. No, no, no, no, *no*. It couldn't-

She hadn't. Not what she-

Whatever she had just witnessed, it was not-

What had she *seen?*

She gulped in large, almost painful breaths against the constriction in her chest. It helped with the nausea, if nothing else. What she had seen could not be. What she had seen was not *human*. What she had seen...

If she put it in context. Framed by every odd thing, every strange remark, every badly-kept secret of the past few days...

She couldn't allow it to make sense. Because if she did, then *nothing* made sense anymore.

Abruptly, she pushed herself away from the tree. Looked around this way and that, but she was alone. When she turned and ran all the way back to town, she

heard nothing but the gentle rustling of the leaves and
her own quick, shallow breathing.

XII

She made her way through Ilmoure's streets more by rote memory than anything else. Even after all those years, she found her way home as everything seemed to pass her by in a blur. Above all, she kept listening, or tried to, for anything out of the ordinary. The sound of footsteps other than her own, the sound of someone following, catching up, and-

She didn't want to think about it.

Iris fumbled her way over the gate and to the back of the house, where she'd left the backdoor unlocked. She slammed it shut behind her, making herself nearly jump out of her skin in the process. But the house was empty, because her family were out there, up in that old mine, doing who knew what with things that should not exist on this earth. It didn't matter that she tripped and stumbled into the bannister. That she cursed as she stood up again, and that her heels created a frantic rhythm on the wooden floors as she hastened up to her room, grabbed what she could find in the light of her bedside lamp and stuffed it back into her bag. Something tore when she yanked her coat from its hanger downstairs, but she couldn't care to check what damage she'd done.

She threw it on, grabbed her belongings, and fled the house she had grown up in once again.

The town felt dead and empty as Iris scurried through its streets, glancing this way and that, into alleys and door- ways and over her shoulder. Every shadow was waiting to jump her, but nothing ever did. Every noise was some- one following, catching up, ready to strike, but nobody was in sight. Iris' heart pounded in her chest as she left Folsom Street, turned left and right and left again on a terrified whim, not sure where she was going, just *away*, away from where she couldn't be.

With every step, the images burned themselves into her memory, digging sharp claws deep into her mind and refusing to let go. Desperate to pretend she hadn't seen what she'd seen, Iris couldn't keep herself from mulling it over, again and again, an obsession.

With every turn, it became more bizarre, more un- moored from what she'd thought to be real – more coherent. It was like all she'd had until now was blank pieces, and if she accepted this one as part of the puzzle, the image finally appeared. An image she would much prefer to forget, but knew she never could.

Of course nobody had told her about Rose. Of course Daniel was out of town. Of course Laura wasn't grieving a son who'd never died.

Every little thing that had seemed so odd now seemed perfectly logical if she accepted that she *had* seen what she'd seen, that it *did* mean what she thought it meant. And if it did...

She couldn't stay. There was no way to leave, but she couldn't stay.

Iris stopped in the middle of the street, breathing hard and fast and ragged. She had to get a grip. Had to keep a clear head and think straight and find a way out.

She looked around. Without thinking, her feet had carried her where she'd always gone to find answers. The library loomed foreboding and dark at this hour, closed to her. She stared at the door. Hide inside? For the night? No way she'd get through the lock. Maybe a window. Or perhaps-

It wasn't difficult to find. Among the townhouses, few offered the convenience of an apartment over the responsibility of the entire building. It was a desperate, foolish hope, but the reward was a name on a bronze plaque, an old door that allowed her inside with little resistance, and a very angry Cateleya, wrapped in a fluffy robe and with the wrath of god behind her, as Iris' hand was still raised from where she'd gripped the knocker before it had been yanked out of her hand.

"What in god's name are you doing here in the middle of the night?"

For a dumbfounded moment, Iris didn't know how to answer that. A thousand reasons ran through her head, each one more freakish than the last, and none would make her sound like a sane person one should hear out. She swallowed thickly, trying to calm her racing pulse, to no avail.

"I need help, Cat. Please."

Cateleya bristled. "It's C-" She fell silent rather abruptly, looking Iris up and down. "You what?" Only now did she seem to notice everything. The bag at Iris' feet, the sweat on her face. Whatever might be lurking in her eyes, she didn't know. "What happened?"

"I... I don't know." Iris raked a hand through her hair. "*I don't know*, it's-" She gulped in a breath. "I can tell you. I can't explain, but I can tell you. Please."

Cateleya looked at her for far too long. Whatever she found, it brought pity to her eyes. It should have rankled. Instead, Iris felt nothing but relief when Cateleya stepped aside.

"Come in."

Iris nearly tripped over her own feet as she entered Cateleya's tiny apartment. There was no entryway, just a cramped little living room with a couch and an armchair grouped around a coffee table, an archway into a kitchen and two doors. One was open to what had to be a bedroom. Just as Iris was about to look away, something moved in there, and she dropped her bag on her own foot.

"Shit!"

"Damn it, Iris! Keep it down!"

Iris stared at the sand-coloured cat that had entered the room and was now yawning enthusiastically. "I thought he was the library cat."

"He comes up with me sometimes. I don't mind."

When Iris turned around, Cateleya had closed the door and crossed her arms in front of her, and was looking very mad indeed.

"Out with it. What in the world is going on?"

Once again, Iris' throat felt tight. She hunched her shoulders. "Can we sit down? It's... I don't know what it is. A lot."

Perhaps if Iris had looked a little more composed, had been a little less desperate, Cateleya would have tossed her out into the street. As it was, the pity never left her eyes as she pointed at the couch.

So they sat. Iris perched on the edge of the armchair, and Cateleya on the couch, with both a blanket and the cat draped over her legs. *Library mascot.* The librarian's mascot, more like.

Iris clenched her hands in her lap. Her fingertips were still a little red and sore where she'd held on to the ledge underneath the church window. "I know how this is going to sound. But I need you to listen, to all of it, because one thing doesn't make sense without the other, and I... I need someone to hear this." She dug her nails into her palm. "I need someone to *believe me*, because I think I might be going insane."

Cateleya narrowed her eyes at her. "All right. I'm listening. Just cut the dramatics, it doesn't suit you."

Iris bit her lip so hard she tasted copper to keep herself from laughing. "Of course." She tried to breathe, calm and steady, and it took a few breaths to loosen that vice around her chest. "No dramatics."

And so she told Cateleya everything. Without dramatics, she recounted it all, from the day she had arrived, the funeral and Laura's smiles, the empty house at night. The preacher and her undignified eavesdropping, how she had followed – and finally, what she had seen, in both the church and later at the entrance to the mine.

"I swear I didn't make this up!" She wrung her fingers, unable to bring herself to look at Cateleya. "It wasn't shadows, it wasn't a costume, they were... I don't know what they were, but they weren't people. Not normal people, like us, like..." She ran a hand across her face. "But those two, the ones that Laura... They looked like her. They looked like *us*. It's the only way this makes sense. Why they lied to me about Rose, why I never saw Laura cry, why Daniel didn't attend his own son's funeral." She exhaled sharply. "If Daniel even..." She shook her head. "I don't know. I don't know how." Finally, she did look up to meet Cateleya's eyes. "I just know that's what I saw."

Cateleya held her gaze, quiet for too long. "Monsters," she eventually said. "Monsters in the mine that look like dead children."

"I know!" Iris raked both hands through her hair, pulling at the roots to ease the pressure inside her skull. It didn't help. "I told you it doesn't make sense! But this is the only way that it does!"

"Now you're talking nonsense." Cateleya wrinkled her nose and raised her hand before Iris could go on, could try again to convince both of them that she wasn't crazy. "I do think you believe every word of this." She ran her hand through the cat's fur, who stretched and purred and was entirely unconcerned by all of it. "You said..." Unease crept into her features. "You saw my father."

Iris twisted her fingers in her lap. "He was at this... this service, or whatever it was. His wife, too." She swallowed thickly. "You always used to go, didn't you?"

Cateleya bit her lip. "I stopped years ago. Father Melville's sermons became..."

Iris sat up a little straighter. "Strange?"

Cateleya nodded slowly, hesitantly. "My father said the church was just changing with the times. He never stopped going." Suddenly, she looked up, a sharp glint in her eyes. "That cross. What did it look like?"

Iris huffed. "It wasn't a cross. It was..." Her hands drew aimless patterns in the air. "Like loops, but with angles. You couldn't really tell how many, it was... hard to look at."

"I see."

Cateleya gently pushed the cat off of her. Breadstick loudly voiced his displeasure, but Cateleya was already in the bedroom. Iris watched the door until she came back, clutching something in her fist. She held it out to Iris.

"Like this?"

Iris stared at the gold in Cateleya's palm. Her heart skipped a beat, then started hammering against her ribs when her eyes traced those odd lines. Like in the church. Like in her parents' salon.

"Where-"

"My father gave it to me for my birthday." Cateleya closed her fingers around the ornament and stuffed it into the pocket of her robe. "He never told me what it was." She sat back down, knees drawn up to her chest. "Did he..."

She didn't have to finish. Iris nodded. "They both went up there."

Cateleya became a shade paler. "To talk to monsters."

Iris perked up, hope sparking weakly in her chest. "So you believe me."

"I don't know."

Iris felt light-headed. It wasn't a no. And yet. "Please. You told me about Rose. Don't you think there was a reason why nobody ever told me? Why they lied when I asked?"

"I have your word on that and nothing else."

But it lacked conviction. Cateleya gnawed on her lip, worried the edge of her sleeve.

"So your sister..."

"Went up there to see her children."

"So you've said."

Abruptly, Iris stood. It startled both Cateleya and the cat, but they remained where they were as Iris strode over to the window.

"I know what I saw. I know what they looked like. I know this is the only way I can fit all of this together to make sense." She stared outside, trying to find a landmark. Her eyes landed on the church, now a dark and empty silhouette, and wandered above towards the trees. She turned to Cateleya. "Look. You can see the paths from here. The road to the mine is just over there." She waved at the approximate spot. "They'll have to come back down eventually. You can watch from here."

"Iris..."

"Please." She hated how she sounded, but she had this one chance. If Cateleya didn't trust her... "Just watch."

Whatever compelled Cateleya to get up, pity, curiosity, or the sheer desperation to get rid of an unwanted visitor, she did join Iris by the window, arms wrapped around herself over the thick robe. Without another word, she leaned against the windowsill and *watched*.

There was no telling how long it would take. Or if they'd already gone back down while Iris had wandered the deserted streets. If they'd already discovered her empty bed, and were looking for her. Her imagination conjured up one scenario after the other, each one more unpleasant than the last. Assigned new and horrifying meanings to everything she'd heard, and the things she'd seen tonight. Perhaps they'd guessed where she had gone, with no way out of the city and nobody else she could trust-

"Oh my god."

Cateleya jolted upright next to her, and so did Iris. Eyes large and luminous, Cateleya was staring out at the dark woods.

Not so dark anymore.

"What is that?"

Bobbing lights, at a pace matching a slow walk – or a procession. They appeared, one after the other, halfway up. They moved together, blinking in and out between the trees as they zig-zagged down from the mine towards the church. Eventually, they disappeared behind the last row of houses. Cateleya followed their slow progress, jaws working and hands digging into the fabric of her robe, until the lights were all gone again.

"Do you believe me now?"

Cateleya stared for another minute before she turned away from the window and pulled the curtain rather forcefully. "I believe that you saw them go to the mine."

Iris growled in frustration. "And why do you think they went there?"

"I don't know! You're telling me it's monsters!" Cateleya paced the length of the room, past the couch and the doors and back again. "How are you expecting me to believe that the reason is '*monsters*'?"

Iris slumped against the wall, blowing out a breath. "I don't know. I really, truly don't know." She rubbed her burning eyes. "But leave that out. I still have my family attending church services at night. They go into the mine that should be closed to everyone to do who knows what, and they don't seem to want me to leave this town again. Isn't that enough?"

Cateleya stopped, arms crossed again, and fixing Iris with a weary look. "Enough for what?" She pinched the bridge of her nose. "What do you want from me, Iris?"

Iris hesitated. What *did* she want? She'd come here running, come for support, for someone to believe her and to confirm that her sanity was still intact. Now though, now that she was safe behind a closed door, away from those things, away from all that madness and whatever her mother and father and maybe even Laura were doing and planning?

She wasn't so sure anymore that she needed all of that. No more than she needed something else, in any case.

"I need help to get away from here," she finally said. "Something is going on, and I want no part of it, but if I stay, I might not have a choice."

Fragments of those conversations came back like needles, painful and persistent. She knew that they hoped she would be like Laura. That she would *stay* and *settle*, like a good daughter was supposed to. And then... Iris wrapped her arms around herself like a shield. She didn't want to believe that. But then, it didn't seem to matter much what she wanted.

"I can't stay, not with this whole town going crazy. But I can't wait, and even if I did, those people on the bus..." She shuddered as she remembered the looks. "I don't think I'll get out of here that way."

"That's all?" Cateleya bit her lip, now red and raw. "You leave town, and then I'll never hear another word about monsters in the mines?"

Iris swallowed thickly. "Your father was there."

"He was always a devout man," Cateleya said brusquely. "What they do during mass is none of my business." She jerked her head sideways. "I can get you to Greenbriar. They have a train station. Tomorrow night. Maybe the day after."

Greenbriar. The line would take her straight to Durham. "Greenbriar is fine." Iris took a shaky breath. Glanced at the front door. "I don't know..." Her gaze flickered around the room. "I don't know where to..."

Cateleya's nostrils flared. "You're not sleeping in my room." She jerked her chin. "You can stay on the couch."

Relief made Iris' knees weak. "Thank you."

"Yes, I rather believe that you should be thanking me," Cateleya said sourly. "After all of your nonsense I should toss you out right now, shouldn't I."

"Cateleya-"

"I already told you to save it." Cateleya pointed at the couch again. "Now go to sleep, and don't bother me again."

And with that, she picked up the meowing cat, marched into the bedroom, and shut the door behind herself with force. Iris flinched, and only when she heard the light switch click loudly on the other side did she exhale, long and weary and taking at least some of the tension out of her shoulders. Exhaustion creeping in now and with nothing else to do, she did as Cateleya had asked, took off her coat and shoes and lay down on the couch. With the lights still on, sleep eluded her despite everything, but she couldn't bring herself to turn them off. If she'd learned one thing tonight, it was that anything could lurk in the dark, even in the safest places. So Iris lay on her back, stared at the water-stained ceiling, and waited for the sunrise.

XIII

T hey spent a quiet and tense hour after Cateleya had woken up – and after Iris had risen from the couch without a wink of sleep – in the kitchen. When Cateleya spoke, it was to ask Iris a question. What had they done at the church, who else had been there, what had the preacher said to her father, what did she know about Rose and Matthew? Iris answered as best she could. Now, when it was light out and she was safe, it should have been easier. Instead, every question increased her inner turmoil, the way she jumped at every little noise and expected the door to be kicked down any second.

Nothing of the sort happened, and soon enough, Cateleya left for work, leaving Iris with nothing but her muddied thoughts and the yellow cat for company. He had chosen Iris' bag as the most comfortable place to nap and refused to leave when Cateleya had stood by the open door.

"Fine. Just don't eat her for lunch."

And with that, she had shut the door and left them to their own devices. Which meant mostly thinking, pacing, and over-thinking, while Breadstick the cat oc-casionally opened his eyes and meowed at her. After the third time, she deciphered the sound correctly and patted his head. From then on, she paced, veered away from the windows, paced back towards the door, and only stopped to pet the cat.

At least it kept her from screaming at the top of her lungs until she felt a little better.

The few times she dared to peer outside, nothing moved in the street. As far as she could tell, nothing moved up in the woods, either, but that might be the time of day. Maybe they only came out at night. Maybe they couldn't walk in sunlight.

She bit her fist to smother hysterical laughter. Vampires. She was thinking of vampires. What she'd seen up there was anything but that.

Probably. Who was she to tell exactly what kind of monstrosity she'd seen.

When the keys rattled in the lock in the late afternoon, Iris flinched away from the window with a strangled noise. She owed it solely to Breadstick looking entirely unbothered that she didn't reach for the nearest thing that might serve her as a weapon. Instead, she waited out of sight from the front door as Cateleya entered the apartment and closed the door behind her.

"Hey."

Cateleya all but glared at her. "Don't remind me." She dropped her purse, hung up her coat, and bent down to pet the cat circling her legs. "How've you been?"

With how sweet she suddenly sounded, Iris decided that the question was not meant for her. She kept her mouth shut, fiddling with the buttons on her vest while she waited for Cateleya to say something. Anything. To tell her whether or not she was trapped in this cursed town.

Finally, Cateleya stood up straight again. "I caught Henry during lunch," she said. "He has a car. He agreed to drive you to the station tomorrow after school."

It was ridiculous how relieved Iris felt after this innocuous bit of news. "Thank you." She worried the chain of her watch. "I would've paid for the bus fare, I can-"

"Tell him that."

Iris watched as Cateleya wandered around the apartment, taking off her shoes, hanging her keys on a hook, opening the window without regard for Iris' unease as she did. Something seemed off about her, different. It bothered Iris that she couldn't pinpoint what it was. Did she talk to somebody? Did she give away that Iris was here? Were they on the way to take her... who knew where?

They were both startled out of this uncomfortable silence when something heavy pounded on the wall. Iris tensed, eyes going wide.

"What-"

Again. Her heart skipped a beat. Not the wall, fool. The door.

"Cateleya? Are you home?"

They shared a glance, Cateleya now looking more confused than angry – for the most part. "My father."

You don't say. Iris frantically shook her head. With a sigh, Cateleya pointed at the kitchen.

"In there, stay quiet."

For want of a better alternative, Iris obliged. She huddled beside the archway, pressed between the wall and the high kitchen cabinet. At the same time, she heard the door handle rattle, and then the hinges creaked.

"Father." Heavy footfalls that thankfully stopped a few steps into the living room. "It's been a while. What is the matter?"

"Am I not allowed to check on my daughter?"

"Check on me?" The door clicked shut, and Iris' heart leapt into her throat. Breathe. Just keep breathing. Even if he noticed, he did not know she'd seen him. "Why?"

"Nothing, I hope." She heard him pace, flinching with every step he took. "I'm sure you know that Miss Grey is in town. For young Matthew's funeral?" He paused, but Cateleya stayed silent. "She has left her family's home rather in a hurry last night. They fear she might be unwell, and…"

"Unwell?"

"Not herself, if you prefer. Grief, perhaps, they don't know. They'd like to know where she is, to make sure that she's safe, and Eleanor thought that perhaps she'd come to you."

Cateleya huffed. "To me? She damn well knows better."

"Language, Cateleya!"

"Spare me, father, I am an adult. I also happen to be very hungry right now, so I will make this short. No, Iris has not been here. She came to the library a few days ago, we were polite, and I have not seen her since." A rustling sound. "Why are *you* looking for her, anyway?"

"I'm trying to assist poor Anthony and Katherine. They are worried."

"Please." Lighter steps around the room. "Iris can come and go as she wants. She probably skipped town. She likes to do that, remember?" More rustling. "So why would you ever think she'd come to me?"

"I assumed that perhaps…" Mr. Belafonte trailed off. Took a few steps. "Cateleya, is that… Are you pregnant?"

It was like something in the air changed. Cateleya's tone was frosty when she replied. "I was going to tell you in a few weeks."

"A few-" Her father made a strange sound. "How…" A moment of silence. "Who?"

"I am quite sure you know who."

"You can not-"

Iris twitched in her hiding spot. Something in his voice made her want to go out and shove him out the door. She forced herself to stay put. Cateleya had it handled. She'd always known how to do that.

"You should have told me," Mr. Belafonte finally said. "Your mother and I-"

"Did not need to know yet."

"*Your mother*," he repeated, "would have wanted you to confide. You don't know... There are things that need to be considered."

"We are considering them," Cateleya said coolly. "Henry is not one to run away, I can assure you. We will be handling the situation."

"The situation!" His heels clacked on the wooden floor. "You! And with him! I would never have thought..."

"Yes, well, neither would I, but here I stand, don't I."

"Yes, you do indeed." In the tense silence, the rattling of the lock was piercing. "There is business I have to attend to. We will talk about this, Cateleya."

"There is nothing to-"

The door opened and closed in quick succession even as she spoke. The moment Iris heard the lock click, she pushed herself away from the wall and peered into the living room. Cateleya was standing by the door, arms wrapped around herself.

"Cat?"

A spark of irritation brought her back to life. "I thought I'd made myself clear."

Iris winced. "Cateleya." She bravely ignored the glare and approached. "Are you all right?"

"I am." She sighed, and her shoulders slumped. "He will be mad for a while, I assume. He might be right. I should have told him. I just thought we should wait until we had decided what to do.”

As tempting as it was to ask, to find out more about Cat’s life after Iris had left her behind, it seemed best to steer clear of that for now. It wasn’t fair, was it, when Iris was about to leave her again.

To what, though, was unsettlingly unclear at this point.

“Thank you. For... Well.”

“Of course.”

It did not sound like it was a matter *of course* at all. Instead, Cateleya abruptly turned, yanked the chain in front of the door, and stalked into the kitchen.

“I need dinner.” She pointed sharply at a cabinet, and the look in her eyes told Iris that it was better to stay silent. “You go and feed the cat.”

If the morning had been awkward, the night bordered on torture. They ate in silence apart from the enthusiastic slurping coming from the floor next to the kitchen table. Cateleya seemed to be just fine pretending that Iris wasn’t even there. When the kitchen was cleaned up and dark, she changed, took a basket from the shelf, and sat in the armchair. She remained focused on her knitting while she listened to a radio drama. Breadstick lounged on the couch taking up most of it. Iris had just about enough space to sit, hold a book, and not read a single sentence as the minutes ticked away.

“I need to ask you something.”

Iris wasn’t sure when the needles had stopped clicking. The drama was pausing, commercials droning in the background. Cateleya was looking at her with doubt in her eyes. Iris nodded slowly.

"What is it?"

"What happened when you asked about Rose?"

Iris' grip tightened around the spine of the book. "Why?"

"Humour me."

"I didn't ask about her by name," Iris admitted. "I went and described that picture you showed me. The little girl Laura was holding. There was nothing. I asked if the child was Audrey's, because she looked so much like us. That's when my mother got... angry? I don't know. She said Audrey left. That she never had children, and I must be mistaken." She drummed an erratic rhythm on the back of the book. "They mentioned her later. When they left the house at night and thought I was asleep. That's how I know they were lying."

"I see." Finally, Cateleya looked up. "I was just wondering, you know? When I went to put away the books this morning, the picture wasn't there anymore."

"How did she find out?"

"We forgot a picture. In the library."

Clearly, they'd taken care of that right away. Iris' stomach churned. "Do you believe me now? That something is happening?"

"I believe you when you say that your family is hiding something," Cateleya said. "I don't know about..."

She looked at the half-finished blanket in her lap. The look on her face was achingly familiar. It had been there a lot during those last few months before Iris threw everything away like the fool she was. Emboldened by the fact that Cateleya had started the conversation, Iris plucked up the courage to ask a question of her own.

"Why was your father so angry?"

Cateleya's chuckle was tired and curt. "Because he's been angry about a lot of things. That I moved out of the house. That I started seeing Henry." A tiny smile flickered across her face. "A man from the city, and one who dresses *like that*, no less." She turned serious again. "That I stopped going to church. That most of all. He kept asking me to go back with him and Eleanor. Insisted that I'd like it. That my mother would have wanted me to go, be involved in the community and all that. Find a nice young man from the congregation to settle down with, I suppose."

"So you went and found a nice, not quite so young man from outside of it." Iris scratched the back of her neck. "I see."

Cateleya huffed. "Oh, that probably stings, too, because I'm not official with Henry in any way, and I'm not sure that I want to be any time soon." She sighed and picked up her needles again. "He'll calm down again. He always does. He probably just had a little shock when he realised that his grandchild would have *my* last name."

Yes, if one was the sort of father to care about that, it must have been. Iris kept a rather scathing reply to herself and opened her book again. She still didn't get much reading done, but at least she didn't feel like she was suffocating in the tiny room anymore. Just one more night. Tomorrow, she'd be on her way back home.

The couch was slightly less than comfortable, and neither the street lights outside the window nor the cat wedging himself between her back and the couch were helping the situation. When Iris woke up from something or other for the third time, she tossed the blanket aside with a huff and padded into the bathroom. The lamp outside was just about enough to see by, so she only fumbled around a little while she did her business, drank some water from the tap, and splashed some on her face to try and get rid of the grainy feeling behind her eyes. It didn't help.

Iris nearly screamed when something banged on the front door. Hands gripping the edge of the sink, she stared at her wide-eyed reflection. Who the hell-

"Cateleya! It's me!"

More banging, fists on wood, and Iris was reaching for the key to unlock the bathroom door when she heard the bedroom door flung open. What the hell was her father doing here at this hour?

"I'm coming!"

Frozen in place, Iris listened as her pulse sped up. The chain rattled, and the creaky hinges signalled that Cateleya had opened the door.

"Is something wrong with-" She yelped, and in turn, startled Iris. "Who are- Father, why-"

"You are coming with us."

"What? What happened?"

"There are things we need to do. You need to come, now."

Come with them? In the middle of the night? Iris reached for the door handle again. The hell they were dragging Cateleya somewhere in the wee hours.

"I'm not going anywhere. Father-"

"You are, Miss Belafonte."

Iris stopped dead when she heard the new voice. Not just her father. More than one. She bit her lip, tasting copper. One, she could get out with a solid punch or two. Two, she was much less certain about handling. She glanced around, too afraid to turn on the light, but unable to see right. A weapon. She needed something that could deal a good whack. Did Cateleya not own a plunger? She pulled open a drawer. Scissors, surely?

"You can come on your own two feet or we can carry you."

Iris' head snapped up. Shit. Shit, shit, shit.

"What the hell? No, don't you- Let go!"

"Stop it, Cateleya! This is necessary!"

"Put me down right now and tell me what the hell-No!"

Someone screeched, and a mess of footsteps pounded the floor.

"Get the fucking cat off me!"

"Leave him alone!"

"Just get her out of here, now!"

"Father? Help!"

The edge of panic in Cateleya's voice spurred Iris into action.

"Help! Help m-"

There was a crash, and Cateleya stopped shouting while Iris somehow managed to jam the key. More footfalls, growing faint. Iris cursed as she wrenched the key free. Then fumbled the lock again. When she finally opened the door, she did so with one hand in a fist and ready to swing.

Instead, she found herself in an empty living room. *Shit.*

She darted over to the open door. She had to step over the wardrobe that had come off the wall, spilling Cateleya's coats and hats into a pile. Iris ignored it and peered outside, left and right. Nothing. Gone already, just like that. And so was Cateleya.

Iris retreated back inside. Pressed herself against the wall. What the hell had just happened?

Insanity, was what had happened. Her own father. Why? What did he *need to do* to his own daughter?

She pushed away from the wall. Couldn't turn off the lights. They'd know. So she stayed as close to the wall as possible as she peered out of the window. Not a moment too soon. They came out the front door, three of them – Cateleya's father ahead. He didn't seem to have a care in the world that one of the others had his daughter slung over his shoulder like a sack of potatoes. She wasn't moving as they shoved her into a waiting car and drove away. Iris wanted to scream.

Instead, she forced herself to consider her options. She needed to find her. Raise hell until everyone in this god-forsaken town knew what was going on behind closed doors in their precious church. Kick down a door or two and drag Cateleya out of wherever they were taking her. Make sure that she was safe.

And probably get herself caught as well, because why else would they be looking for her, too?

She turned away from the window, raking her hand through her hair. She couldn't leave Cateleya like that. And she couldn't trust anyone. If Cateleya's father would do this... If her own family were involved...

Who was there for her to turn to?

XIV

As she jogged down the street, armed with nothing but desperation and a pocket knife, she was, for the first time in years, tempted to pray. If only she knew that what would answer wasn't what she'd seen up at the mine. Or worse.

She turned every corner with her heart in her throat, only to find the streets as empty as they always were. In front of the schoolhouse, she came to a stumbling halt, clinging to the desperate hope that she was right.

The sign was paper, taped to the bronze plaque underneath that marked it as the teacher's apartment. Either he didn't expect to stay, or this was their way of letting him know that they didn't want him to. Either way, Iris nearly sobbed in relief when she smashed the door knocker into its metal plate. He would help. He had to.

Iris almost fell over when the knocker was yanked from her iron grip. She just about caught herself before she crashed into him and knocked them both to the floor.

"What in the world is going on?"

Henry Mason sounded equal parts grumpy and surprised. Not even a little bit panicked. Iris gaped at him.

It seemed absurd in the face of *everything*. She had to remind herself that he didn't know.

That he had to know.

"Iris, what are you-"

"I need your help." She pushed past him and shoved the door closed before he could do more than yelp. "They've taken Cateleya, and the entire town has gone crazy, and you're the only one I trust not to hurt her."

His face remained blank as she turned around. "What?"

"Did you not listen?" She just about had the good sense not to shout. She needed his help, not get thrown out of his house. "They took Cat! I don't know why, they didn't say, but they took her in a car, and I need your help to get her back!"

"They... took her?" It was like a jolt went through him; he seemed a lot more alert now. "What's that mean, they took her? Who is they? What happened?"

Iris blew out a breath and took a step back. Good. He was listening. That was good. "I have no damn clue what any of it *means*. I was staying with her for the night, and her father came by her place..."

It didn't take long to recount the events that had led her here. With every word, Iris was increasingly aware how absurd it all was. How it had to sound to him, who hadn't seen what she had, and who hadn't known her nearly long enough to take her word for any of it. But he did listen. Confusion gave way to anger as he did, and when Iris was finished, he looked rather ready to throw a punch or two.

"Her own father?" He made a low, guttural sound. "I knew he wasn't happy about us, but I didn't think..." He ran a hand across his face. "I don't understand." He focused sharply on Iris. "And I understand even less why you are here, and not down at the constabulary. If he's kidnapped his own daughter-"

"Because I don't trust anybody anymore," Iris cut him off. "I know how it sounds. I know you don't believe a word of what I said about those..." She shook her head. "I saw too many people at the church. Too many important people. If I talk to the wrong person, I'm done for, Cat's *gone*, and nobody will ever know."

"And so you came to me because...?"

Iris huffed. "Because you're sleeping with her, and you're not from around here. You were my best bet." She swallowed thickly. "Tell me I wasn't wrong about that."

"I-" Another one of those noises. "We can't just run after them. Where would we even start looking? I doubt she's at his house, he could have just invited her for dinner and she would've come on her own." He raked a hand through his hair. "So you don't trust anyone in town? We could drive down to Greenbriar. Talk to the constable there. Have them come up and-"

"Greenbriar's an hour there and back," Iris argued, "if we can even get anyone there to listen. I'm not going to leave her with him a minute longer than I have to."

"You don't even know where she is!"

"I..."

Iris fell silent. Didn't she? He wasn't entirely wrong. If they hadn't taken her to her family home, then where was she?

Her head snapped up. "You wanted to know what happened to those kids."

He took a step back. "What? I... What's that have to do with-"

"He came after he learned she was pregnant."

Iris started pacing in the tiny hallway, because standing still was not an option, because oh god, she knew where they had taken her, now. It finally clicked – who had gone up to the mines. Parents, children, and the two women who were so prominently pregnant. It couldn't be coincidence.

"Whatever it is had to happen quickly." The question was – why? She *did* know where, though. "She's either in the church or up at the mine."

"And what do the children have to-"

"Because I saw them." She held his gaze and refused to back down. "I saw Matthew, I saw Rose, both of whom you and I know should be dead, and you *still* came to my father's house to ask about him. And now they take children up to the mine in the middle of the night?" She poked a finger at his chest. "You knew something wasn't right. Here's your chance to figure out what that is, and help me save your girlfriend while you're at it!"

"She's not my-" He shut his mouth abruptly, like everything else she'd said registered a little late. "What do you mean, you saw your nephew? He died, he-"

"Was up there hugging his mother like nothing ever happened."

"You said these people looked like some kind of frog creature!"

"Well, maybe that's why they never come back to school!"

He stared at her, open-mouthed. "You realise that you sound quite insane, right?"

"So call the asylum in the morning if you must!" she snarled. "Until then, are you helping me find Cat or not?"

She fully expected him to take her up on that offer right this moment. That she'd have to get out and find Cat on her own. Instead, he looked her up and down like he'd just realised she was there. He turned abruptly and walked towards the stairs. "I will need a few minutes to get dressed. We will check the church and the mine, and if she is not there, I *am* going to the constable, and you should consider not being there anymore when I return."

It was madness, really, but what did that matter when the whole world seemed to have gone mad right alongside you?

They walked in silence, at a brisk pace, but not nearly fast enough for Iris' liking. She kept a firm grip on the pocket knife in her coat. It was all she had, and he had even less. She'd asked if he had a single thing to arm himself with. He'd refused to even take the poker from his fireplace. Iris had known better than to push it. She might need him more than she realised at this point.

She hoped it wouldn't be so, but then, she'd hoped for a lot of things in her life, and she rarely got what she wanted. So she was determined to get at least this. What came after, they'd sort out when Cat was safe again.

With Iris taking the lead, whether or not he liked it, they arrived quickly at the churchyard. Here, they trod more carefully. Perhaps he did it because he was inclined to believe her after all. Perhaps he had simply decided to humour her. She refused to look at him as they darted across the graveyard, next to the paths to avoid making noise.

The church was as dark and empty as Iris had feared. The front door was locked. When Iris clambered back up to peer through the window, she only saw the empty pews, and the odd altar with the chalice and the knife in the middle.

"So? Everything is normal, I presume?"

She bit back a scathing response as she dropped down. Turning to face him, she had half a mind to chew him out for dithering when Cateleya needed their help. Instead, she held her tongue and stepped aside. "Take a look at the altar."

"Iris-"

"Just do it, will you!"

He scowled at her, but ultimately complied and stepped on the outcropping. Iris watched him closely – and saw the moment the tension crept into his body.

He glanced over his shoulder. "Is that-"

"Knife and chalice, on an altar that very much does not belong here? Weird symbol where the cross should be?" Iris crossed her arms. "So you do admit that this is not normal?"

He dropped down with a thud and a wince. "I don't know. I'm not exactly a god-fearing citizen, but I do know this is not what a church is supposed to look like." He looked around, too, now. "This is where Cat's father goes?"

"He was here last night. He didn't go up to the mines, but..."

He looked at her expectantly. "But what?"

Iris tried to ignore the knots in her stomach. "My sister did. Her and another woman. They're both pregnant. They were first in the... line, I suppose." She caught his eye. "She's up there now, I know she is."

He took a shaky breath. "I... concede that you may have a point. We need to get to that mine."

Relief made Iris' knees weak for a moment. This was all she needed. He'd see. God, he'd see. "Let's go."

XV

T he forest was so dark they barely saw where they were going, but it couldn't be helped. They could not risk being seen, and this way, they'd know when anyone was getting close. Still, Iris had to remind Henry to be cautious. By now, he seemed almost more eager to reach that cursed mine than she was.

Though they both slowed when the crowns of the trees thinned out, granting them a little more light as they approached the mine. They stuck as close to the side of the path as they could, and Iris was glad for it. It allowed them a split second to duck behind one of the bushes as a shadow moved up ahead, in the dim light of the lanterns next to the mine's entrance. A guard.

Iris shared a glance with Henry. She softly shook her head, then looked around at her feet. Rock in hand, she waited for the guard to turn his back as he paced back and forth, then moved up just a little, motioning for Henry to follow. He did, just in time. The guard paced back, stood still. And stood. Iris felt her grasp on her patience slip just when he turned again abruptly. They moved up once more. Iris threw the rock.

She flinched as it not only rustled the bushes thirty feet away, but smacked into something solid with a loud thud. Her heart leapt into her throat as the guard spun around to face the sound – and raised a gun at it.

"Hello?" A beat. "Doyle?"

They stayed silent, waiting, and Iris had to force herself to keep breathing. Bit back a squeak when the man started moving again – away from them, and towards the treeline opposite. She glanced over her shoulder.

Now or never.

They tiptoed past as fast as they dared and dove into the open entrance to the mine. The inside was mercifully unguarded. Iris wracked her head, but couldn't recall whether or not she'd seen a guard last time. Maybe they'd posted one just in case she was dumb enough to return here.

In fairness, she did indeed seem to be lacking in the common sense department. It just hadn't worked out for them the way they probably thought it would.

They didn't speak until they were well past the first few bends. Here, they slowed their progress as they followed the cart tracks deeper inside. Small lamps were hung on the walls, just close enough together to create continuous light. The tunnels that branched off were dark, black pits just beyond the threshold for all Iris could see. It didn't matter. If they didn't maintain them, they wouldn't be using them. This one would lead them to Cat.

"Iris?"

"Yes?"

He exhaled sharply. "When we find Cat, you need to take her back to Durham with you."

Iris slowed momentarily, only picking up her pace again when he nearly bumped into her. "I need to what?"

"If she's in here, she isn't safe in Ilmoure." A pause. "She isn't safe regardless, but she'll never listen. She doesn't want to leave, and believe me, I've tried. You'll need to convince her."

"Like she'll listen to *me*," Iris murmured. She took a deep breath; then again, she did agree with him whole-heartedly. "I'll do my best."

He was an optimist, he really was. Iris preferred thinking ahead a step at a time right now. Otherwise, she might just scream. First things first – and first, they had to find Cateleya.

The means to do so presented itself shortly. At the end of the tunnel, they found a little nook with a doorframe that looked like it might have been an office, once. Next to it, an elevator.

It was a rickety old thing, unchanged since long before the mine had closed down. Space enough for half a dozen people, if that much. The sign above the grate closing it off was so old it was looking green in the dim light. Whichever number had once been on it had been scratched out and replaced with a two. Probably reasonable, all things considered.

"Let me just..." Henry slipped past her and pulled the grate aside with surprisingly little noise, then peered inside. "I'd say ladies first, but give me a moment."

When he stepped into the elevator, Iris resisted the urge to yank him back out by the collar. The contraption made a dreadful sound, but it held. Slightly encouraged, Iris swallowed her anxiety and joined him. She winced when the cables groaned and the metal creaked.

"Lovely." She pulled the grate closed and squinted at the lever next to it. It, too, had an old sign, and it had been amended as well. *Storage 1. Storage 2. Worship.* Iris paused. *Deep.* She rested her hand on the lever. "Let's try them one by one."

The elevator cage rattled, the cables groaned some more, but before Iris could even begin to regret her decision, they descended into pitch-black darkness. Without a single source of light inside the elevator, all they had for company was each other, the creaks and groans of the cables, and the mounting anxiety over what they would find when they got back into the light.

If there was any light down there at all.

Iris swore. How had she not thought of that? If they needed light, and had none-

"Something wrong?"

"We might need a lamp down there."

He was quiet for too long. "I have a lighter."

Well. It was a start. At the very least, it might allow them to look around, and return to the elevator to...

They'd figure that out if it got that far.

Iris' heart skipped a beat when she finally saw a faint glow edge its way into the elevator from below. She hardly had time to prepare for whatever they might find when the rock wall gave way to open space again. Nothing pounced on them from the shadows as they did. Iris still craned her neck to cover every possible angle as she pushed the grate aside and stepped back onto solid ground.

"Looks clear."

True to the sign, it really seemed to be some kind of storage area. The space was oddly large for a mine. The differences in the wall texture suggested it had been expanded. Possibly to fit all of the wooden crates that were stored in here, in neat, straight rows from one end of the room to the other.

Henry stepped off the elevator and stood next to her. "What in the world would they store inside a mine like this?"

Iris looked around, hesitant to touch any of the boxes. "Beats me. If it's not Cat in one of these, I don't care."

"They're not nailed shut." He approached the nearest crate. "Let me see."

Iris watched as he cracked open the lid. A second later, he let out a low whistle.

"Gold."

"What?"

She hurried to join him, peering inside. The dim light gleamed off a pile of oddly shaped…

Nuggets. Gold nuggets the size of a chicken's egg.

"That can't be gold. The mine ran dry before I was even born."

He cleared his throat. "You mean, besides the fact that mines don't produce nuggets?"

Iris barked out a humourless laugh. "You think this is the most bizarre part of this?" She left the crate be and moved on, slowly, checking the next one, and the next. The same. In every single one. "I have no idea where this is from, but it's not mined. If it was, why would they hoard it down here instead of reopening the mine?"

"I'd love to ask, but something tells me I wouldn't like the answer."

Wasn't that right. There had to be an explanation for this, but Iris shuddered to imagine what that might be. If it wasn't the mine, then where did they get all of this from?

As Iris moved through the space, she found the names written on the larger ones, too – Richardson, Meyer, García, Stockton. Further down the row, she recognised more of them. Family friends, neighbours. The exact neighbours, she realised, whose houses looked so neat and freshly renovated. The ones that had, somehow, defied the fate that had befallen the rest of Ilmoure. Now she knew how.

Iris walked along the rows, reading each name with mounting dread. In the end, when she found the ones she'd been looking for, she barely had it in her to feel anything. Audrey McNamara – the cousin who, supposedly, had left Ilmoure years ago. Her box was full, and two smaller ones sat on top, only marked with initials, but equally filled to the brim. Ice in her veins, Iris checked the next cluster of boxes. Still numb, she read the inscriptions. She'd known. Had expected the big bulky boxes bearing the names of her father, her mother, and Laura – that last one, too, was stacked with smaller ones bearing only single letters. Two were filled just like the rest – M and R. And the last one sat empty, still unmarked.

"Damn."

Her head snapped up, and she found Henry staring up and down the other row. "What?"

When he looked up, he looked ghostly pale. "These are my students."

"What?"

"The names. They're all here. Every student that left school, and I was told not to worry about."

Something dreadful fell into place, a ghastly image forming. Every student that had disappeared. Like Matthew, which had had Henry investigate. Matthew, whom Iris was now sure she'd seen, alive and well and something else entirely, just like his little sister.

Iris stared at the small boxes – the *initials*.

Payment. The gold was payment.

Her head snapped up, and she spun around to find Henry. "Is there a box for Cateleya's father?"

"What?"

"Does he have a box?"

Henry looked up and down his row. "It's right here."

Iris hurried to join him. A chill ran down her spine when she saw it – the two smaller boxes on top. One empty and unmarked. But the other was filled to the brim, and the lid marked with a large C.

"What the fuck."

Iris stared at it. That wasn't right. If these were for the children they had with those...

Why did Cateleya's father have one for his daughter?

"Iris?"

Iris tried to breathe against the vice around her chest. "I don't know where the gold came from, but I think I know what it's for." She glanced at her sister's crate, and the damning evidence. "They're being paid for... expanding the family. With them. Those *things*. The small ones, they're for their children. My sister had one for each of hers."

"For..." He fell silent as horror dawned on his face. "No. That can't be it. That's not possible."

"If you'd asked me last week, I would have agreed."

It was the only explanation she'd been able to come up with. But if she accepted that, if she stuck to this logic and what it all meant... It made sense, twisted, awful, disgusting sense. That Cateleya had never known her mother. That her father had been paid for her existence. That he had panicked at the idea of her having a child outside of his control.

But Cat couldn't have known. She'd never have sheltered Iris if she had. Wouldn't have been kidnapped by her own father. Iris turned abruptly around. "We need to find her."

He caught up to her at the elevator. "They're not going to hurt her and the baby, are they?"

Iris bit her lip. Hurt them? That might depend on one's definition of 'hurting'.

"Not if we get her out first," she finally said and pulled the grate closed with a metallic snap.

The next storage floor was just as deserted. Here, there were only a handful of boxes, all empty and unmarked. Unlike the other floor, this one had more tunnels branching off; most pitch dark, some with lights inside. They followed those into adjacent areas – shafts that ended in solid rock walls, a niche full of shovels, pickaxes and buckets, metal rusted over and wood rotting away. The last one felt odd as they progressed into it. Soon enough, Iris realised why – there was a dull murmur echoing off the walls. She stopped, and so did Henry. They shared a look, and Iris had to restrain herself from pulling out the pocket knife. As it was, the murmur did get neither louder nor quieter. Eventually, Henry nudged her and nodded ahead.

What Iris had at first mistaken for a black patch of floor revealed itself to be a hole in the ground. An almost square shaft, with a ladder running up and down. Iris peered upwards into blackness. Down, she could see light.

Light, and shadows moving in it.

"...preparations?"

"Patience."

Iris froze. The voice was familiar, but the echo made it hard to place.

"...know until tonight. It takes time."

"It might already be too late."

"That may be so, but then we will ensure that she is prepared for the next attempt."

It sounded so eerily familiar, and still all Iris knew that she'd met the man before somewhere. She did not recognise the other voice at all – a woman, she couldn't tell more than that.

"She will resist."

"Then we shall have to convince her that it is for the best." The following pause was poignant. "The child will ensure her compliance either way."

"Father."

The third voice cut in, and the puzzle fell into place. Iris bit her lip, cursing that preacher and whatever ungodly abomination he might worship.

"What is it?"

"You'll need to finish the preparations."

"Very well. Make sure everything else is in place by the end of the consecration."

The shadows moved, and footfalls clacked along the rocky floor, the echoes growing fainter with every step. Iris knelt next to Henry, motionless, staring down the shaft until all was quiet below. Only then did she allow herself to breathe freely again.

"They'll take her baby."

His voice was barely a whisper, but Iris heard the seething anger regardless.

"They'll take her baby, and make her..."

He fell silent. He didn't know what they were doing to Cat any more than Iris did. It did nothing to diminish the fury etched into his features. He leaned forward, and after a moment, swung his legs over the edge of the shaft.

"What are you-"

"She's down there."

"Wait!"

He didn't wait. Heart in her throat, Iris watched as he descended the rickety ladder, the rungs creaking and groaning under his weight. But they held, and when he was standing safely on the ground again, he looked left and right, craned his neck, then looked up at Iris and waved.

Praying that their luck would hold, Iris went to follow him down to what the sign had called *Worship*.

Iris' feet had barely touched the ground when the ladder shuddered under her hands and dropped almost a foot. Iris bit back a scream and caught it just before it slammed into the ground.

"Shit."

Slightly dizzy, she strained her ears, but nobody came running. She gently lowered the now broken ladder to the ground. No going back up that way.

"Come on."

Henry had gone ahead, waiting for her at a corner, pressed against the wall. Iris followed, taking stock of their surroundings as she did. Down here, there were no crates, no dim electric lights humming softly in the silence, nailed to crude shaft walls. Here, the walls were smooth and dark, almost polished. Lanterns had been hung in intervals of ten feet, flames flickering and lending the area a brightness it didn't deserve. In between the lanterns, the symbols were hung – shining gold, gleaming in the light, and more than just what she had seen inside the church. All manner of knots, curves, angles and rings, each one different than the last. A small fortune all by itself, never mind what else was stored above. *The city is doing just fine.* Her father's words were making a frightening kind of sense now.

They remained unnoticed for the time being, but they were far from alone. From further down the largest tunnel, they could hear voices, a low, ominous lull. They shared another glance, and followed it.

With every agonising step, Iris expected someone to notice. To realise that the elevator was not where it was supposed to be. That there were intruders. Instead, they were allowed to sneak through the tunnel, peer into adjacent ones and find them empty, find themselves in front of locked doors they couldn't open without noise. They left those be, and eventually came up on a brighter area up front. Here, they got more cautious. Stuck to the walls and slowed down until they were just close enough to the next bend that they could see what lay beyond.

It looked like the church, but not. It had the trappings of one – an altar, the large golden symbol above it that was so difficult to look at, even rough-hewn benches to serve as pews. It couldn't have fooled anyone. Whatever worship happened here did not involve any sort of god. A single look at the people inside confirmed that.

From the corner of her eye, Iris saw Henry clamp a hand on his mouth when he realised what he was looking at. The... people, the creatures, the things that should not exist standing among the townsfolk. The drone was louder here, but it was difficult to make out details. Whenever Iris saw one open its mouth, what came out between those needle teeth was no speech she had ever heard. After half a minute, she realised that they were not blinking.

But whatever they were, it paled against what she saw behind the altar. At first, she'd thought *statues*, large, made from silver-grey stone and adorned with gold jewellery. Then, one of them moved, a slight turn, nothing more, and the light reflected off its luminous eyes. Iris took half a step back. It was enormous. Even in the cavernous space that had clearly been expanded, the odd feather-fur on its head was brushing the ceiling.

It took Iris too much willpower to look away. To scan the crowd of people and not-people for Cateleya and her father. One, she found. The other, she did not.

But someone else caught her eye.

She was standing nearby, with their parent's backs towards the entrance, and the small creatures next to her. The picture was that of a family, the way they'd always looked on Sunday picnics and afternoon walks.

But those children should not exist.

They should leave. Cateleya was not here. If only Iris could bring herself to move.

The small thing that looked like a niece she'd never met reached up to touch her mother's arm. Laura smiled down at it – ruffled the odd hair on its head like it was the most normal thing in the world. A strangled noise escaped Iris before she could help it. Laura raised her head, her parents turned, and Iris flinched behind the bend, back into the shadows.

Shit.

She shared a horrified glance with Henry, and they began the slow creep backwards. Desperate to get away, more desperate to stay quiet. Maybe nobody had seen. Maybe they'd attributed it to the light.

They made it back into the main tunnel when they hard the footsteps behind them. Lips moving in a silent curse, Iris ducked into the nearest side tunnel, pulling Henry with her. Pressed against the wall, they waited. The footfalls came closer, then passed them by.

They stopped.

"Hello?"

Iris bit her lip until she tasted copper. Laura. Whispering. It still echoed, overlapping now.

"Iris?"

She wanted to move deeper into the tunnel. How far was Laura? Would she hear?

"Please. I need to go back before they look for me."

In the looming darkness of the tunnel, Iris closed her eyes and rested her head against the rock. It sounded... sincere. And she hadn't screamed. Hadn't shouted for attention. Had come to meet them alone.

Come to meet her.

Iris gulped down her fear with little success. Glanced towards Henry and put a finger to her lips, hoping he would catch the hint. Then, hand in her pocket and fingers wrapped around the handle of her knife, she stepped out into the light.

"What the fuck is going on here, Laura?"

Her sister flinched and turned around, eyes wide. In the strange light down here, she looked so pale. The dark dress didn't help. She looked almost pathetic, if Iris ignored the reason why she was here – and what she had just seen.

"Iris. I-" She looked up and down the tunnel. "What are you doing here?"

Iris exhaled sharply. "Is this a joke? I'm here for Cateleya."

Laura flinched. "That's not possible. Please, Iris. You need to leave, now. There's nothing you can do."

Iris' blood ran cold. "What's that supposed to mean?" She took a step towards her sister, who flinched. "What is going on, Laura? What is this? Who are these... What are these? The *things* you..."

Treat like your children.

An odd flash gleamed in Laura's eyes, and she drew herself up with her chin raised. "They're not things, Iris. They're our salvation. Our benefactors."

Salvation. Like the god they had replaced. Iris tried to find something, anything, in her sister's features when she said that.

"They're monsters."

"They're our partners!" Laura flinched once more when her voice echoed further down the tunnel. She ducked her head. "You haven't been there. You don't know."

"Then fucking tell me!"

Laura shook her head. "I can't. There's... It's too much. We don't have time. Please. You need to leave."

"I'm not leaving without Cateleya." Iris' fingers dug into the metal edge of her knife. "She's here. She has to be. Her father took her, and he was right there with those-”

Iris bit her tongue, trying to suppress the part of her that wanted to scream, to shout and to drag Laura out of here. That desperately wanted her to explain, to tell her what in the world she had witnessed, and how any of it made sense.

That was not why she had come here. That was not something she could do.

“Where is she, Laura?”

XVI

The silence was oppressive, and with every heartbeat, Iris' hope faltered. Why Laura was here, she didn't know. If not to help – would she sell them out after all?

They both flinched at the footsteps, and Iris almost drew her little knife before she remembered that she hadn't come alone.

Laura stared at him, face white. "What's he doing here?"

Iris almost laughed. "Same thing I am."

"Iris." Henry looked between the sisters, distrust so evident in his eyes. "We have to go. If she's not helping us, we need to find Cat and-"

"I know." Laura gulped audibly. "I know where they brought her. They want to..." She pressed a hand to her mouth – and the other to her belly. "It's hard, to carry them healthy. She's never had any support, so Father Melville is going to administer it tonight. In case she... To help her."

"Help her?" Iris took half a step back. "How the hell is this supposed to-"

"It's her baby." Laura reached out, grabbing Iris' arm so quickly it startled them both. "If she's... If her heritage comes through, she needs assistance. Please. She could-"

"What heritage?"

Iris wouldn't have considered him an aggressive man, but with how Henry got right into Laura's face, she found herself reassessing.

"What's wrong with her baby?"

Her sister's eyes were large and luminous as she looked between Iris and Henry. "Her mother. She got it from her mother."

"Her mother? What does her mother have to do with..."

Iris stopped listening when it sunk in. When all the pieces snapped together into a revolting picture. She yanked herself free from Laura and grabbed Henry's shoulder.

"She was one of them." She held Laura's gaze, daring her to object. "That's why Cat never met her. She didn't die. She was one of those... whatever the hell they are."

"Ascended ones," Laura whispered. "They ascend, and so do we."

"I don't fucking care." Iris forced her words into a hoarse whisper, or else she'd scream and bring everyone down on them. "They're not going to do jack shit to Cat. So you can tell me where she is, or you can fuck off back to your *family*, but we're not leaving here without her."

Iris would have expected many things. Cursing. Shouting for help. Maybe a healthy slap.

Not tears.

"I'm sorry." Laura sniffed, wiping her eyes. "I didn't want you to come. When she told me she'd already sent it. You weren't supposed to be here at all." Her breath hitched, and Iris flinched, glancing down the tunnel.

Someone had to notice by now, didn't they? "You need to leave."

Iris squared her shoulders, trying to ignore the quiet sobs. "Not without-"

"I know." A strangled little sound. "I'm so sorry. I'll take you. Take her and go. Promise me that you'll go."

"We were planning on it," Henry replied brusquely, for both of them. "Where?"

Laura stared at him for a moment longer, then turned abruptly. "Follow me."

She stalked away, up the tunnel. Iris almost ran after her, only just catching up when Laura stopped by one of the side tunnels. Her sister was kneading the seams of her coat, making them creak and loosen with every twist and turn. She looked over her shoulder, tears still on her face.

"Down here."

It wasn't far. This one looked more orderly than some of the others, too. Unlike the room near the elevator, there were doors in here. Thick, wooden ones, with tight grates covering vertical slits in the top half. Laura knocked on each one. By the third, she stopped, almost stumbling. She righted herself, leaning close to the grate.

"No, it's fine. Cateleya, it's me. Laura? I'm with-" She winced, and Iris could hear hearty swearing from inside. "Please stay quiet. I'm with Iris and your... boyfriend."

The swearing abruptly stopped. Something thudded against the door. "Iris?!"

Iris all but shoved her sister aside. "It's us!" She pressed her face near the grate, finding Cateleya's on the other side. "Are you all right?"

"I don't know." Cateleya was breathing too fast, too shallow. "I don't know what's happening. My father- He said-" She gulped in a breath. "I saw..."

"I know." Iris forced herself to take a step back and examine the door. "I know. We'll get you out." The door was thick, heavy, and they had no tools. "Is there a-"

"It's not locked." Laura hiccuped. "Just a bolt."

It was. Laughing in relief, Iris reached for the thing, thick and rusty and resisting when the pulled.

"Shit." Iris' grip slipped, and she tried again. "Come on…"

She yelped when she was unceremoniously shoved aside. "Let me."

It took Henry a mere few seconds to pull the bolt sideways. It crunched along with difficulty and more noise than Iris liked, but the door swung open, and out stumbled Cateleya. "Henry?"

"Thank god." He wrapped her in an embrace, just long enough for Iris to wish she could be in his place. "Are you all right?"

"I…" Wide-eyed, Cateleya looked between them all. "What is happening? They said I needed to wait, but I don't know for what. Where are they?"

"Probably looking for us." Henry took a step back. "We need to go. Now."

Noise grew louder as they approached the main tunnel. As they stepped back into it, Iris' heart skipped a beat. Footsteps to their left. Dancing shadows too close. No time to lose.

Henry set off, with Cateleya at his side. Against all reason, Iris hesitated. Held out her hand to Laura.

"They'll know." Her gaze flickered to the back of the tunnel. "Laura, please."

The heartbreak in Laura's eyes hurt even now. She hadn't understood. Of course she hadn't. She was one of them – but was she?

"I… I can't!"

"You have to! What do you think will happen when they realise you helped us escape?"

Laura's lips trembled. Iris still held out her hand. Something in her sister's eyes went dark. She fell to her knees with a heart-wrenching sob.

"Laura-"

Her sister looked up at her, and Iris knew she had lost. "Just go!"

Chest tight, Iris did. She ran, swelling voices behind her, like tidal waves come to drown her. At the end of the tunnel, the elevator just moved into view as she caught up with Cateleya and Henry. Cateleya seemed oddly unmoved as Henry was pleading with her to get inside.

"They're coming." He laid a hand on her shoulder. "Cat, please."

"My father." She was looking between them, down the tunnel. "He never told me…"

"Oh, for the love of…"

Iris wedged herself past Henry and shoved Cateleya into the elevator. She stepped inside right after, squeezing into a corner to make room. She turned to find Henry still outside. Cateleya leaned towards the open grate.

"Henry?" A spark returned to her, and her voice gained an edge. "Henry, come on!"

Henry looked up, then back over his shoulder. Finally, at Cateleya.

"If it drops, we're all done for." Before either of them had time to react, he leaned inside and cranked the lever all the way up. I'll be right behind you."

Iris flinched when the elevator groaned to life and started moving upwards, the grate still open, as Henry took a step back. Next to her, Cateleya moved, and Iris just about managed to wrap both arms around her.

"Henry? Get in here right now! Henry?!" She lunged again, pulling them both to their knees as the elevator's ascent plunged them into darkness, and Henry disappeared from sight. "You fucking liar! *Henry!*"

There was a shout, a woman's scream, and then the noise below disappeared underneath the rattling of the elevator. Cateleya suddenly went limp in Iris' arms.

"He lied," she whispered, leaning against Iris. "He fucking lied."

Whether she meant Henry or her father, she never said, and Iris didn't ask. She just knelt next to Cateleya, listening for any irregular noises, and looked up to where their salvation was waiting.

And a guard.

"Shit." Iris scrambled to her feet. "Cat, get up."

A hacking wheeze in the dark. "What?"

"Get up. We're not out of the woods yet."

The mine itself was still deserted when they emerged into it. After she'd dragged Cateleya out of the elevator, she turned around and pulled the grate half closed before she yanked on it as hard as she could. The metal twisted with a shriek, sticking half out and half in. It wouldn't hold forever, but with any luck, it'd buy them a few precious minutes until the mob down below got it working again.

This, unfortunately, did not go unnoticed.

"What the hell is going on in there?"

The shadowy figure that entered sounded more annoyed than vigilant. Which might have bought Iris the seconds she needed to reach into her pocket and take out the knife. Blade extended, she hurried to meet the man half-way.

She'd never seen him before in her life. So when he realised she did not belong to the congregation, it was too late. He'd raised his gun, but it never fired a shot as Iris stuck the tiny knife exactly where it would do the most damage.

The man sputtered as Iris pulled the blade free again with a twist, eyes wide in fatal surprise. His weapon clattered to the ground and warm blood gushed over Iris' hand as he swayed and stumbled.

"Iris-"

"We need to go."

Iris dropped the knife like she'd burned herself. Wiped her hands on her suit, again and again, which only served to make her nauseous as the blood seeped through instantly.

Shit.

Shit, shit, shit.

"Cat, we need to go."

"You..." Cateleya shuffled past the convulsing man, back against the wall. "You-" She stopped, eyes wide, to look at Iris. "Henry-"

"Can meet us in town. Come on!"

Cateleya did not argue further. In fact, she took the lead as they jogged through the woods, down the path and towards the lights of Ilmoure. When they reached the paved roads again, slowing down ever so slightly between the looming houses left and right, she turned the corner back to her apartment. Iris held her back by the arm.

"Where are you going?"

"My place."

Iris shook her head. "We're leaving town."

"I need to-"

"Cat, they'll find us!" She looked at her former lover, who seemed like little more than a ghost floating next to her in her nightdress. "We have to-"

"I need some fucking shoes, Iris!"

Iris flinched. Right. Shoes. Stupid to walk around in the dark barefoot.

So they took the stairs two at a time. The door was still open. Cateleya disappeared into the bedroom, not without pointing at the sideboard. A purse on top. Two drawers, some cash in one, papers in another. At the bottom, a letter with her own name on it, in the corner for the return address. Iris stared at it, just for a moment, before she took it all. She hadn't sooner stuffed everything into the purse when Cateleya appeared again. Shoes on her feet, like she'd said, an armful of clothes, and delicate metal dangling from her fists. She dropped it all on top of Iris' open bag, then stalked towards the door.

She took her best coat on the way out.

They darted from corner to corner, avoiding the lights as best they could. There was noise now. Coming from the woods. Closing in. They were running out of time. Cateleya, though, seemed to have reached an odd equilibrium. Like she had a goal in mind, and without any ideas of her own, Iris followed and hoped for the best.

They'd never closed the door to the teacher's apartment, either. Beyond caring about who saw, Cateleya flipped the light switch. Rummaged through the chest of drawers. Made the strangest little sound when she held her prize aloft. A set of keys, shiny and new and modern.

"Let's get out of here."

Henry's car, a boxy, black thing so unlike the sleek new models cruising Durham's streets, rumbled along the road in the dark. There should have been lights, but Cateleya hadn't found them. Instead, she'd cursed, sobbed, and said it was better that way. At least they'd have to look harder.

Between Iris' feet sat the purse and her bag, open, topped with what little cash and jewellery Cateleya had to buy her way to a safe place far away from here. The change of clothes thrown haphazardly on top had fallen off from the motion of the car. Just as well – it served as a very fancy bed for the skinny yellow cat curled on top.

"What's he doing here?"

Cateleya stared at the animal perched on the hood of the car, meowing loudly as if to welcome her back. "I don't-" She'd reached out and yanked him off the hood so quickly Iris could do nothing but grab the cat that was thrust at her a second later. "You hold on to him."

So Iris had. Breadstick the library mascot had swatted at her for her troubles, but she'd held on, if not for the hissing animal, then for Cateleya. Cat, who was driving them too fast for the winding road, away from Ilmoure and what lurked beneath at a pace that should have had them flying off the road ten times over. Cat, who had not stopped to wait, who had run ahead back to town, whose only thought had been to *run, run, never come back.*

Maybe that was her way of saving at least one life besides her own from whatever dark pit of secrets Ilmoure had become.

They ran out of gasoline half a mile away from Greenbriar. Silence hung thick and heavy as a coastal fog between them as they walked to the train station in the growing light, Cateleya's grip around Iris' hand like steel. The cat, incredibly, chose to follow them of his own accord. It was the only time Cateleya spoke – she insisted they buy a basket, a tin of food, and some water for him at the first open shop they could find. Breadstick seemed quite content with this. When they sat down in their compartment, blissfully alone, he began to snore just as the train started to move out of the station.

Cateleya, seated opposite Iris, hands folded primly in her lap like this was any old day trip, stared out the window, all but unblinking. Only when the dense rows of houses had changed to little cottages and then to bushes and trees did she finally find her voice again.

"What now?" She turned her head, catching Iris' gaze. Her eyes looked flat and hollow. "What are we going to do?"

Iris wished with all her heart that she had an answer. A plan, steps they could follow and check off a list and know that safety would wait at the end. A solution, not another mess to deal with. She looked down at her hands, with nails rimmed dark and a network of rusty brown lines dried in the ridges and valleys of her skin. Why were her hands so dirty?

"I don't know," she finally said. "I'm sorry. I don't know."

Cateleya raised her hand to her mouth, but the sob came out regardless. Ugly and desperate, it opened the floodgates. Moments later, Iris found herself sat next to her, holding her, trying and failing to find something, anything, to say to make it better.

She couldn't make it better. Could not console a daughter so betrayed by her own kin. Fix the loss of her child's father. Or even begin to explain how, why, maybe, that child...

If her heritage comes through. If.

Maybe. But maybe not. She couldn't know. And now was not the time to question. They could do that later. Could sit down and talk and maybe find someone to help. Find someone who would do what they couldn't, who would go in and tear out this black growth at the heart of their home and fix it.

If there was anything left to fix at all.

"It'll be all right."

She kissed the top of Cateleya's head as her eyes began to burn. Outside, the horizon was glowing pink and orange and beautiful.

"We'll be all right."

XVII

I ris entered the constabulary at noon with an hour to spare. The starkly illuminated space was quiet this time of day. A handful of people were milling about, and most did not spare her more than a brief glance. Iris approached the man sitting behind the front desk. It took him a moment to finish what he was writing and look up.

"Can I help you, ma'am?"

"I would like to report a possible crime." Iris tried to keep her hands still. "It concerns the disappearance of several children."

"I see." He neatly stacked the papers in front of him. "Please elaborate?"

"I've heard from the town's teacher that his students will leave class and not come back. Whenever he inquires about them, he is met with vague answers. Nobody will tell him what happened to the students." A flicker of a glance at the large clock at the wall. "Mr. Mason has also been out of touch for some time now. I fear something might have happened to him, too."

The man froze minutely. "I see." When he rose, with a smile on his face and a glint in his eyes, the light caught on something pinned to his lapel. "And where are these disappearances taking place?"

"In Ilmoure." Iris stared at the small pin, the loops and angles of gold against his grey suit. "That's north of here."

"Ilmoure." He nodded, and his smile grew teeth. "I am familiar. Please follow me. Someone will take your statement."

He turned and headed down a windowless corridor leading deeper into the building. Iris stared at his back. When she turned and headed back towards the door, she heard his footfalls stop.

"Ma'am?"

She pushed open the door and took the stairs two at a time.

"Ma'am, come back!"

At the corner, Cateleya was waiting, two suitcases and a wicker basket at her feet and her hands in her pockets against the chill air. Her coat didn't quite close anymore. She inclined her head at Iris' approach.

"That was quick."

Iris picked up the suitcases. "They know what they need to know."

She waited for Cat to pick up the basket. From inside, Breadstick the cat whined a nasal meow that told everyone within earshot what he thought of his accommodations. It brought the tiniest smile to Iris' face, brittle as it was.

"Come on." She marched into the crowd, towards the station. "We've got a train to catch."

THANK YOU

Thank you for sticking with my story until the end!

If you enjoyed it, please consider leaving a review on Goodreads or the storefront where you purchased the book. Reviews mean a lot to independent authors, and each and every one supports us in bringing you more fantastical worlds, intricate mysteries and wild adventures in the future.

Also consider following me on social media or signing up for my newsletter on my website to stay up-to-date about future releases!

Twitter: @CaraD_author
Facebook: @CaraNDelaney
Instagram: @carad_author
Website: caracatcheswords.wordpress.com

ACKNOWLEDGMENTS

A heartfelt thank you to my online communities, both the writing ones and the non-writing ones. To everyone who patiently explained something to me that I could not figure out how to google. To the people who have listened to me rant about unimportant details at two in the morning. You put up with my silly questions, my one-sided brainstorming and my frustrated venting. From the bottom of my heart, thank you for all of that. My work would be a lot harder and a lot more lonely without you.

And the biggest of thanks to my family, who don't mind not seeing me for days at a time, and who never complain when lunch is quick and easy so I can get back to work.

You're the best support an author could possibly wish for!

ABOUT THE AUTHOR

Cara lives in a hole in the ground, where she spends her days building whole worlds with nothing but words on the page and a lively imagination.

She may be summoned with a potion brewed from magic beans, but there is no telling what will happen if you do.

Once in a blue moon, you might catch her out and about on a walk through the local vineyards, soaking up the sun and taking pictures of trees.

c/o Block Services
Stuttgarter Str. 106
70736 Fellbach
Germany

Cover by www.covercreator.uk

ISBN: 978-3-910588-01-1

www.ingramcontent.com/pod-product-compliance
Lightning Source LLC
LaVergne TN
LVHW010529200726

843506LV00013B/2752